Yvette twisted around on her hands and knees to peek through the tiny rear window of her carriage as the other drew closer.

She soon recognized the large black traveling carriage with four enormous horses adorned with white feathers, pulling it along. No matter how much she might wish it were any other, it stopped not far behind hers.

Her coachman rushed to approach it, speaking first with the servants and then to the occupants within. The carriage door burst open, and Luc Ayles emerged dressed all in a black. Great coat snapping about his long legs.

Yvette's heart sank as she collapsed onto her seat. She was about to be rescued by a scoundrel.

By the biggest scoundrel of all.

HEATHER BOYD

USA TODAY BESTSELLING AUTHOR

LET IT SNOW

Other short works in print by Heather Boyd

In the Widow's Bed
Love Me Tender
Love Me True
A Husband for Mary
A Ramshackle Start

The characters and events portrayed in this book are fictitious. Any similarity to real persons, living or dead, is purely coincidental and not intended by the author.

LET IT SNOW © 2021 by Heather Boyd
Editing by Kelli Collins

Chapter One

December, 1813

"Lord Middleton, you're giving me no choice but to strenuously refuse your advances again," Yvette Valiant said to the gentleman holding her just outside the ballroom door, before kicking his shins and scurrying back into inside to the smothering warmth and stench of the house party guests.

Not that anyone seemed to have noticed she'd just had to save herself from being imposed upon by a scoundrel.

Here, that was a frequent occurrence.

She took a deep breath, pasted on a smile that should fool everyone but her best friend, and weaved through the crowd, looking for her brother, her chaperone at this wicked house party.

For heaven's sake, she had just wanted one gulp of fresh air, not immediate molestation! Why her brother dragged her from Bath for this depraved amusement, she didn't know. Did he want to have her ruined and married off to someone she would hate for all her days?

She searched for her brother and found him propping up a marble pillar on the far side of the room. She returned to the dubious safety he offered, hoping no one questioned where she'd been. But she couldn't miss another opportunity to point out his shortcomings.

"Where were you when I needed you?" she hissed to Rhys, head of the family now and all-around annoyance since her birth. He was three years older and ought to know better than to leave her unchaperoned here.

When he didn't answer, she noted the direction of his attention was upon the other side of the ballroom. Given the way he was smirking, the one relation she ought to be able to place her faith in for the protection of her virtue was much too busy considering how to rob another young lady of the very same thing. She deliberately stepped on his right foot. "Rhys."

"I haven't moved all night, Yvette," he protested with a brief glance at his abused foot. "You're the one who keeps running off."

"I danced, and since I was thirsty, followed Lady Pillsbury to the refreshment table since you refused to accompany me." She stared at him in vexation. "Do you even care to know what became of me after that?"

Rhys patted her shoulder. "I trust you," he said with calm unconcern before smiling at a different lady as she promenaded past.

She failed to prevent her hands from curling into fists. "There are too many scoundrels here," she hissed, and then looked around guiltily.

Being around her brother for any duration tended to bring out her shrewish side, unfortunately. It was all she could do not to strangle him some nights.

"There are scoundrels everywhere, or so you insist," he noted. "If I thought the company of my friends so dangerous, I'd never take you anywhere. Besides, you'd never let a scoundrel actually catch you, so why should I worry, too?"

He is so right about not letting myself be caught by any scoundrel.

Yvette was most definitely keeping her virtue for marriage by any means possible. There would be no hushed-up scandalous marriage like some of her cousins had engineered for themselves. Someone in her family needed to adhere to a higher moral standard.

It constantly disappointed her that the family reputation was not the best, despite her brother's promises to reform. She had no hope that the rest of her family could ever change.

She'd been well aware of the family scandals even before she'd come out. Her late father had kept two mistresses before his untimely demise at the hands of an overwrought half-plucked goose and a garden pond. The goose, desperate to escape the cook's knife, had charged at her father and his lover. Father had, by all accounts, gallantly put himself directly into the path of the goose and borne the brunt of the unprovoked attack, but in doing so toppled them all into the pond. Father hit his head on the marble pond surround and had drawn his last breath with his face nestled between his lover's ample breasts.

And if that was not enough shame to bear in her first season, there was her widowed mother —kicking up her heels on the continent with the family gardener as her new lover.

She shuddered. Her brother, as much as she'd worshiped him growing up, seemed determined to break hearts left and right—including hers.

Given the disreputable reputations of her illustrious relatives, society stalwarts had viewed her with a wary eye when she made any overtures of friendship. It had taken all of her first season just to prove herself someone worth acknowledging and to make just one true female friend.

And despite her rigid adherence to decorum, ignoring all scoundrels and rakes, unfortunately, a good marriage had proved elusive. But the number of scoundrels circling her each night of this dreadful house party had continued unabated. She could not wait to leave tomorrow morning.

"How long must I stay here?" she asked in a whisper, but Rhys was already bored with talking to her and was looking elsewhere.

She considered stomping on his toe again.

"Where would you rather be, Miss Valiant?" a deep-voiced gentleman asked instead.

Yvette straightened her spine as Mr. Luc Ayles, her brother's longtime friend, moved to stand at her side. She wished good manners didn't dictate that she had to look at him to give a response. He was alarmingly handsome and the most dangerous scoundrel that might ever have lived. With his pale hair too long and rakishly falling across one gray eye, she could easily see why he appealed to a certain type of woman.

But not to her.

Yvette was immune to rakes and scoundrels and any man without honorable intentions. Luc Ayles certainly did not have those.

"Right here," she lied, wishing with all her might that Mr. Ayles would single out another woman to attempt a seduction. He'd followed her around too often at this house party for her to have any patience left for him. "I am afraid I have somehow turned my ankle," she murmured.

"Probably happened when you kicked Middleton in the shins just now," Ayles muttered quietly, eyes flashing with mirth.

If anyone heard Middleton had almost caught her, or that she'd assaulted him to free herself, she'd have everyone thinking that she was to blame. "I did no such thing!"

"He undoubtedly deserved it." Ayles nodded.

"A pity you cannot dance. I had persuaded our hostess to play another waltz. You enjoy twirling, don't you?"

She did. She shrugged to hide how sorely disappointed she was. "I will have to wait until next season."

"I was afraid you'd say that," he murmured, eyes full of laughter still. "Perhaps next year."

"Perhaps," she murmured without looking him in the eye. Yvette tried to avoid committing herself to dancing with any scoundrel, especially Luc Ayles, though he was remarkably persistent in asking again and again. Out of the corner of her eye, she spotted Rhys drifting away without her. "Good night, sir."

Ayles held her back a moment. "I was hoping you would allow me the privilege of your company for sledding tomorrow."

Hell could freeze over before she shared a sled with Mr. Ayles again. The first week of the house party, he'd tried to steal a kiss, and with her brother just twenty feet ahead of them. Rhys hadn't heard the slap she'd been forced to administer to the scoundrel standing with her now.

Yvette fluttered her fan before her face, as if she was blushing, but in truth she was fed up with Ayles' dogged pursuit. She had tried to make her disinterest in him plain and painless from the start, but obviously he could need a hammer applied to his head before the message sunk in. "Perhaps we'll meet again at another winter party some other year."

"Yes," he drawled, and then he laughed. "I thought you'd say that, too."

She was about to leave him, but the thing was—and it pained her to admit—she could not be mean to him without feeling bad after.

"Happy Christmas, Mr. Ayes," she said with a broad smile, holding out her hand to him.

The scoundrel sidled closer and looked down at her outstretched fingers. After a moment, he clasped her hand and attempted to bring it to his lips. She resisted.

"Happy Christmas, Miss Valiant. I hope our paths cross again soon."

Not if I can help it. She smiled sweetly, extracted her hand and hurried after her brother, who had cornered her best friend.

"Charlotte, there you are!" She squeezed herself between Rhys and Lady Charlotte Beckham because Charlotte was already blushing badly at whatever he was telling her. "Would you fetch Charlotte and I a glass of punch, brother?"

Rhys hesitated but gave in to her demand when Charlotte whispered "*please.*"

When he was gone, Charlotte let out a shaky breath. "I know you won't agree, but I swear your brother is just as much a scoundrel as my cousin Luc."

"After this house party, I'm inclined to think

all men are scoundrels," Yvette muttered, then remembered to flutter her fan before her lips. "Are there no decent men left in society?"

"If they are, they're not here," Charlotte noted. "Perhaps that's why so many ladies set their caps for rakes. There's nothing else for it but to reform one."

"Some men are beyond reform." Yvette caught sight of her brother on the other side of the room, now talking to a lady with a terrible reputation for being a wanton. She sighed. Rhys had likely forgotten about getting them that glass of punch. Probably the moment he'd turned away and spied a woman alone. "Can you imagine the effort it would take to reform a rake? The frustration? The headache?"

"Hmm, I think I feel one coming on now," Charlotte said, raising her fingers to her temple.

Yvette turned back to her friend immediately "Are you really getting another so soon?"

"Unfortunately, yes." She sighed. "I haven't had a thing to eat all day. Mama insisted on another fast."

Yvette drew near, worried for her friend's health. Charlotte's body was of rounded proportions, but no amount of fasting had ever done more than given her headaches and a tendency to faint. Charlotte needed food immediately, but there was no food to be seen at this hour usually.

She caught hold of Charlotte's hand. "We'll

have to brave the dangerous halls together and find you something."

Charlotte nodded, clutching Yvette's fingers tightly. "You are a true friend."

They weaved through the crowd, making sure Charlotte's mother did not see them slip away.

They reached the hallway, and someone large and male brushed past them. "Ladies. Come with me."

It was Mr. Ayles again, dogging her steps again. He disappeared down a darkened corridor.

She and Charlotte glanced at each other, but he returned quickly. "Food is this way, Charlotte."

Charlotte nearly ran to him, and reluctantly, Yvette followed her into a candlelit room far from the ballroom and any appropriate chaperones, too. But there was food and drink heaped upon a small table. More than enough for two.

"Oh, I could kiss you," Charlotte cried as she rushed to the table and put a napkin on her lap.

"Please don't," Ayles begged, holding up his hands to ward her off.

"You are a lifesaver, cousin," Charlotte said and then fell to eating as if she hadn't done so for a week.

Ayles nodded. "I will speak to her about this again," he said in a voice so hard and cold, it raised the hackles on Yvette's neck.

"She won't listen. She never does." Charlotte swallowed and quickly sipped her tea. "But thank you for the feast. This should rid me of my headache soon."

"Choose a husband quickly, cousin," he urged.

Charlotte giggled. "You did say *you* wanted a wife."

"Not you, Charlotte. No offense." He glanced toward Yvette. His jaw clenched and then he said, "Lock the door to keep the scoundrels at bay when I'm gone."

And then he left the room swiftly, brushing past Yvette and only leaving the scent of his cologne lingering on the air. Charlotte made sure the door was locked and then went to sit by her friend as she ate. "Are you feeling better now?"

"Getting there." Charlotte paused in her eating. "If only my mother cared about me half as much as my cousin always has. He's the only one who tries to help, but he's not always around."

Yvette was surprised by her praise for Luc Ayles. "Does he do this often? Bring you to food-laden tables."

"Oh, yes. All season in fact." Charlotte sighed. "He's a scoundrel through and through, I grant you that, but he's so kind to me. I do hope he marries soon."

"What?"

"Yes. I knew you'd be surprised. He promised

me he would wed soon, and when Luc marries, he will also invite me to stay with him and his new wife in London. Mother is sure to let me go if she won't have to bear the expense of another season. The trouble I cause her, always wanting to eat twice a day," she joked, but it was truly no laughing matter.

Yvette poured Charlotte a second cup of tea and considered Luc Ayles' chances of making a good match. Someone good enough to befriend Charlotte. "What lady would want to marry your cousin?"

"Any number, I'm sure, given his reputation with the ladies." Charlotte sampled another sandwich, grinning impishly. "He's devilishly secretive about who he wants to marry, but he has told me in the strictest confidence that there's only one lady on his mind. I suspect, too, that I know her. The trouble is, I just cannot figure out who she might be."

"So, a friend already perhaps," Yvette mused, feeling a pang of unreasonable worry that Luc's future wife might not be good enough for Charlotte.

Charlotte suddenly met her gaze with wide eyes. "I ought not to have told you about his plans to marry. You mustn't tell anyone. He'd be cross with me."

"I won't tell a soul," Yvette promised, but her mind whirled. "We share many of the same friends, Charlotte. I wonder who it could be?"

Charlotte nibbled on another sandwich. "I don't suppose you'd consider marrying him?"

"No," she said firmly.

"A pity. We'd have all gotten along very well, I think."

Only if Luc Ayles wasn't a scoundrel.

Chapter Two

"There you are again. Pure torture and tempta-
tion for any scoundrel," Luc complained under
his breath as he fixed his eye on Yvette Valiant
standing in the entrance hall with just the one
slightly built maid lingering by her side. She
ought to have ten around her by rights. There
were wagers aplenty at this house party on who
might have the elusive beauty in his bed. "But
don't move a muscle, sweetheart. I mean you no
harm."

Timing was everything when it came to pur-
suing devilishly skittish women. He'd never met
another lady who could look at him for half a
minute and know precisely the moment he'd
imagined her writhing naked either.

Every man here looked at Yvette Valiant that
way, too.

Dark blonde hair, perfect rosebud lips meant
for kissing, a trim and somewhat athletic figure.
If not for her strict adherence to the proprieties,
infallible intuition and a wicked hard kick, she'd
likely have been ruined long ago. Her brother
was no use as a chaperone.

Luc, a *terrible scoundrel* in her eyes, had tried

not to like his best friend's younger sister for quite some time. He had even tried to be offended by her attempts to *politely* insult him, but instead he'd been charmed.

Now her first season was over…he'd found his interest in Yvette had not waned one iota.

He'd been doing his best to protect her from other scoundrels while attempting to advance his own cause. But he had not done well so far. Attempting to engineer ways into her company without anyone, even Yvette, knowing what he was doing, hadn't produced any noticeable improvement in his appeal.

He was probably bound to fail, but he would not give up yet. There was still time to charm his way into her affections before some other scoundrel succeeded in claiming her.

Luc didn't want Yvette to end up married to someone who might never care about her. That was the way his parents' marriage had gone. And the way Yvette's parents' marriage had started had been less than ideal, too. Both of them had horrid parental examples to follow and, to him, it seemed they had that burden in common.

His fixation on her was odd, though, when she offered him no encouragement. He'd never met a woman so offended by the sight of his face. He'd been assured by numerous lovers that his handsome face, together with his other skills, made him a highly desirable lover.

But that was in the past. He'd turned his back on wickedness. Yet, winning Yvette's trust was a slow business that required extreme patience on his part.

However, for the present moment, he had an advantage.

As of an hour ago, her brother, his best friend and hopefully future brother-in-law, Rhys Valiant, had been snoring his head off in his bed-chamber upstairs...and *still* being the worst chaperone imaginable at a house party made for sinners.

Valiant's frequent inattention to his sister was highly predictable and had afforded Luc opportunities for prolonged conversation with Yvette so far. Anything beyond good morning or good day was a vast improvement on their interactions during the height of the season. This morning he ought to have at least ten extra minutes of conversation with her before she remembered her missing brother and begged to be excused.

Luc tugged down his waistcoat and fiddled with his coat sleeves before strolling out to where he could be seen by her. As usual, she scowled immediately. But he didn't let that divert him from the mission of his heart.

He smiled broadly as he approached and offered a court-worthy bow. "Pray is that you, Miss Valiant?"

Yvette looked as if she'd sucked on a lemon.

Thanks to her habitual good manners, she couldn't ignore him without appearing rude. "We are about to leave, sir," she said in a clipped tone.

"We?"

"My brother and I are on our way home to Bath today."

Damn it to hell. Why hadn't Rhys told him they were to go early from the house party? He would have had his valet pack his belongings. He'd no reason to stay if she were not here, too.

He affected a smile, but he was seriously worried. He likely wouldn't see her again until well into the new year. "I'd better wait with you. I must speak to your brother about him leasing my townhouse next season."

Her brow furrowed. "But won't you need your townhouse?"

"I hope to spend much of the warmer months in the countryside next year," he told her. "I've also promised my grandmother to stay with her awhile. She is getting on in years."

A confused expression crossed her face. "What about Charlotte?"

"Charlotte?"

"She said something about her staying with you and your...well, for the season?"

Luc kept his surprise from his face with extreme effort. What was Charlotte doing, telling Yvette about his plans to marry? Did she want to scare her off? "She told you I've a mind to marry."

"She told me nothing, and she couldn't very well stay with a bachelor."

"No," he said slowly, watching her face. "Once I'm married, it is my hope that my wife will agree to chaperoning Charlotte until she finds herself a husband."

That seemed to appeal to her, because she was nodding now. "You'll need to keep your London townhouse if you want to help her wed," she suggested.

He nodded. "I had not considered that, but thank you for the reminder."

The silence extended between them. Yvette kept glancing up, no doubt hoping her brother might appear. Valiant *had* consumed a great deal of brandy last night. Finally, she glanced his way. He received a tentative smile. "I want to thank you for what you did for Charlotte last night. That was very kind."

"It was nothing."

"I had no idea her mother was restricting her diet so often," she admitted.

He nodded, but the last thing he wanted to do was talk about his aunt's nasty habits. Aunt Gael, Charlotte's mother, was a vain, self-absorbed creature whose daughter had been starting to gain too much attention this season. Aunt Gael took out her dissatisfaction with her own fading looks on the poor girl any way she could. Making Charlotte starve herself was just one way to share her misery and make his cousin self-conscious about the generous curves she was born with.

There was nothing wrong with Charlotte that he could see. Her curves paired well with her sunny personality. She'd make any man a good wife.

But not *him*.

Luc's interest remained on the young lady standing at his side who probably wished him far away.

She wet her lips. "I wonder what's keeping my brother."

"Perhaps he is still asleep."

"No." She glanced up the staircase, and a frown formed on her face. "He could not be. He promised we'd leave at nine o'clock."

Luc rubbed a hand across his jaw to hide his pleased expression. Rhys had no sense of time passing normally. And since he had consumed so much drink last night, there was a good chance he was feeling the effects still today. Rhys routinely broke promises. Had Yvette not thought to check her brother was prepared to leave before making ready for her departure? "Now I think on the matter again, he never mentioned leaving to me. Are you sure he said he was leaving at nine *today?*"

"It was most definitely today."

"He was still in the drawing room when I retired around three o'clock."

A frown line appeared between her brows and her lips pressed tightly together as she likely started to fume. "Three o'clock?"

Luc nodded, only to watch her cheeks turn pink with anger. Never a good sign. "Yes, about that time I think it must have been." He pointed to a curtained bower in the nearby drawing room. "He was deep in discussion with our hostess over on the love seat in the corner when I left."

A flicker of disapproval crossed her face at the mention of their hostess, a wanton creature who enjoying flaunting her lovers under her husband's nose. "I see."

"Yes, I'm sure you don't need me to paint a more thorough picture of what likely came after I took myself off to bed," he murmured. Poor Yvette should never have been brought to this place.

A look of disgust crossed her face.

"*I* slept alone," he hastened to add.

"*I* hardly care what you do or with whom," she assured him with a defiant tilt of her chin.

Luc almost laughed at her haughty pose. She was going to keep him on his toes as her husband. "Are you sure your brother actually told you he was still leaving today?"

She fell silent, but her jaw clenched and un-clenched along with her small hands.

"Rhys might be at breakfast," he suggested quickly. "He never travels on an empty stomach. Would you like me to go and see what is keeping him?"

"No. That will not be necessary. I'll rally a servant to find him and remind him I'm waiting. Excuse me." Yvette hurried off, and soon after a servant fairly sprinted up the staircase from the direction of the breakfast room.

He hoped it would be a fool's errand and that Yvette might remain just one more day, so he might try to charm her again.

When Yvette did not return immediately to the hall, Luc strolled to look out a front window of the nearby drawing room.

The Valiant carriage stood out on the drive out front, being loaded with traveling cases despite the falling snow. The horses and men restlessly stamped their feet, impatient to be off. They'd soon put the carriage away and have Yvette's trunks returned to the lady's bedchamber until tomorrow.

Just to be sure all was in order for their continuing stay, Luc hurried up the main staircase and along to his friend's chamber. Upon opening the door, he was hit but the rumble of a snoring man and the stench of stale gin tainting the air. On looking at the bed, he hastily averted his eyes when he spied a feminine leg sticking out from under the covers.

He quickly shut the door upon the scene. Yvette would be in a temper if she'd seen that, and that would not help his cause at all.

Luc stalked toward the head of the staircase, hoping to head her off and perhaps calm her down if he could. Perhaps he ought to send Charlotte to her as well.

"Come along," he heard Yvette say. "This has been one experience I'd rather forget."

Luc quickened his steps down the stairs, only to see Yvette and the maid stride out the front door, which slammed shut behind her.

He rushed to the front door and yanked it open again.

Through eyes stung from the blast of cold, he saw her carriage depart.

Damn Rhys. Damn her impatience. She couldn't possibly mean to leave without her brother.

But she was.

Again.

He suddenly remembered Yvette had lost patience with her brother's tardiness and had left a London ball without him, too.

She was doing it again, now.

Only this time she'd be traveling a much greater distance without Valiant's dubious protection to safeguard her precious virtue. His eyes were drawn to the horizon where dark clouds were forming, signally a worsening of the weather ahead.

He had to stop her, turn her back, and he hurried out into the cold and down the drive, calling for the carriage to stop.

But they were too quick, or they had been told not to heed his calls.

Chapter Three

Everyone made bad decisions once in their life. Usually, the end result was not life-threatening. Yvette stared out of the family carriage to the white landscape beyond and shivered.

Ceaseless, freezing snow lay thick upon the ground and fluttered down around her unmoving carriage.

Given the number of colorful oaths flying through the air outside, the men were having no luck at all getting the carriage moving again. And they had been making such good time, too.

They were, she fervently hoped, too far away to make going back to that dreadful house party likely. She simply couldn't return to that horrible place. After leaving Mr. Ayles in the front hall, she'd gone upstairs to her brother's room. Her brother was a disgrace, having a woman in his bed and the door unlocked, too. But upon backing from the room, she'd been grabbed by Lord Middleton and almost dragged into *his* bedchamber!

No proper lady should be expected to endure such vulgar importuning.

So, she'd punched Lord Middleton in the nose and *left*.

On her own, with just her maid.

Rhys, the lying, useless scoundrel, could find his own way home to Bath, however and whenever he cared to show his face again. She was done hoping he'd ever be a better man and brother.

There was a rapid tap on the coach door, and she found the new coachman wanted a word with her. She nodded and opened the door a crack but was still attacked by a blast of frigid air. "It won't come good, my lady. We'll have to send a groom on horseback to get help. There's an estate just a few miles ahead."

"You think?" Yvette quaked at the idea of anyone riding off in the midst of the blizzard they'd found themselves in. She shivered, fighting to combat the cold by will alone, but she was afraid. When she'd set off, there'd been no indication they'd be heading straight into a snowstorm of such vigor. "But what about you and the men? You'll be frozen solid out there."

They couldn't all fit in the carriage with her and the maid.

"We'll do all right if we stand close around the horses and stamp our feet until help arrives. If you could just wait here until then, I—" The coachman suddenly turned his head and squinted behind them. "Oh, thank heavens. Another carriage is coming along the road."

"Do you think they could help us? What if they get as stuck as us?"

"Let's hope they're more familiar with the road than me," the coachman muttered and then hurried away to meet the carriage.

Yvette twisted around on her hands and knees to peek through the tiny rear window of her carriage as the other drew closer.

Her maid was already there, her face nearly pressed to the cold glass of the window. "That's a very big carriage, miss. I wonder who it could belong to?"

But Yvette soon recognized the large black traveling carriage with four enormous horses adorned with white feathers, pulling it along. No matter how much she might wish it were any other, it stopped not far behind hers.

She watched as her coachman rushed to approach it, speaking first with the servants and then to the occupants within. The carriage door burst open, and Luc Ayles emerged dressed all in a black. Great coat snapping about his long legs.

Yvette's heart sank as she collapsed onto her seat. She was about to be rescued by a scoundrel.

By the biggest scoundrel of all.

Yvette pulled the blankets tight to her chest, filled with defeat. "Of all the men in England to come along, why did it have to be him," she all but wailed to her maid.

Yvette's maid shifted back under the covers. "At least it is someone sure to know what to do."

Yvette bundled herself under her rugs, made sure her maid was covered up, too, and stared morosely across at the vacant seats opposite, listening as the conversation suddenly became clearer and closer to where they sat shivering.

"This is unacceptable," Ayles shouted. "You are not even on the road to Bath!"

Because she gasped at his observation, there was a mumbled reply she didn't quite catch. Yvette had specifically told the new coachman to take her to Bath and to make all possible haste. The new man must have gotten them lost.

"If you were in my employ, you'd be turned out for this," Ayes announced in such a deadly tone that even she was momentarily afraid for the coachman.

"I am so very sorry, sir. But there's nothing else I can do about it now, is there? The carriage is stuck fast."

"I'll be the judge of that." There was a long pause. "Are the women comfortable in there? Warm enough?"

"I believe so, sir. She hasn't complained."

"She ought to after the danger you've put her in."

There was a pause, and Yvette felt eyes on her, but she refused to turn.

"How are the horses bearing up with the cold?"

"I'm starting to worry about them, to be honest."

"Right," Ayes said slowly. Yvette risked a peek, but all she saw was a pair of wide male shoulders under a back great coat blocking her entire view and a hint of pale hair lying upon the collar. "I think we'd best move your mistress to my carriage, lighten the load on this one and see if we can't get you free and at least off the roadway first."

Despite knowing Ayles was going to turn to speak with her, Yvette felt extremely nervous about it. He was going to yell at her, too.

When the knock came on her window, she jumped in fright anyway.

"I know you have excellent hearing," Ayles said, though his words were muted by the glass. "Gather up your valuables and be ready to make a dash for my carriage."

She glanced up and met his stormy gray eyes through the glass. He was furious, and she instantly rebelled at his demand. "Do I even get a say in this?"

"No, you don't," he said in a tone of forced restraint. "Your men are turning blue while you dither."

That was enough to make Yvette swallow her pride, grasp her reticule and sewing box, and hold tight to her favorite blanket. She shuffled toward the door, and the maid did the same, ready for the blast of cold that would envelope them the moment the door was opened.

Ayles caught her eye and then raised one of his eyebrows. "Ready? One at a time."

She nodded as Ayles wrenched the door

open. Despite Yvette having two good legs and a healthy constitution, Ayles swept her into his arms, held her tight against his chest, and shut the carriage door on the maid to keep her in whatever warmth remained.

"I can walk," she squeaked, kicking her legs.

"You could catch a chill, too, easily," he warned. "I'm also keeping your feet dry."

He strode to his own carriage through deep snow and a groom snapped open the door. She was helped inside, urged to wrap herself up in any blanket, then left on her own again.

Although she tried to see what was happening to her own carriage, she could not see very much as the snow began to fall even thicker.

She cast her eye around her. The carriage of a scoundrel appeared much the same as anyone else's. But Ayles was wealthy enough to have spared no expense or luxury inside. The seats were soft beneath her hands and covered with a rich blue velvet upholstery. An earthen pot filled with hot bricks had been placed on the floor. She stretched her hands to it, regretful that it seemed to have lost most of its warmth.

A few of Luc's possessions were scattered across the facing seat. A book and, to her surprise, reading glasses sitting atop.

She snatched them up and held them to her own eyes, but everything just became blurry. She couldn't picture Ayles wearing them. She'd only ever seen him looking like a scoundrel without.

She quickly put them back as she'd found them. Just in the nick of time, too, for the next moment the carriage door opened, and her shivering maid was helped inside. Then a large figure joined them both.

Ayles.

"Isn't this a damned nuisance," he cursed softly.

"What is it now?"

"The wheel cracked. The carriage is free, but it's not going anywhere for quite some time in this foul weather."

She clenched her hands together to hide her shivers. "What will I do? I cannot stay with you."

Ayles threw another blanket over her knees, and the maid's, too. "I think you have no choice but to be my guest."

The carriage shook and loud thumps could be heard overhead, and she looked up.

"I've taken the liberty of retrieving your luggage," he drawled.

"What about my men? The horses?"

"We'll be a bit weighted down more than I like, but we all should reach shelter by nightfall."

She glanced outside. The shortest day was almost here, and the moon was in decline now. Although it was only the afternoon, they might have an hour before it was fully dark. "Where are we?"

"Didn't you hear?" Ayles' jaw clenched. "Your coachman wasn't heading toward Bath, he carried you *away* from it. He was heading for Loxley Downs."

She gaped in horror. "Loxley Downs? But that is where Lord Middleton's estate is?"

"Yes, I know. Your brother's new coachman was easily bribed."

"I cannot go to Lord Middleton's estate!"

"But it would be warm there, miss Valiant," the maid murmured.

Luc eyes narrowed on her maid, who fell silent immediately under his scrutiny. "I'd be surprised if your mistress wanted to visit the scoundrel's home, given the way Middleton chased her for the past week."

"Of course, I would never visit a scoundrel's household if I had any other choice in the matter," Yvette promised.

Mr. Ayles shrugged. "It's Middleton or me."

Yvette could have wailed like a banshee fighting the certain death of her good reputation.

Not to *his* home.

Not the home of *the* scoundrel.

She had tried so hard to avoid him, and now she had no choice. Middleton wouldn't give up pestering her if she were under his roof. Ayles might not be much worse, but she had to place her trust in someone. "Yours."

Ayles tapped on the roof and the carriage moved off. It slowly passed her own broken-down carriage and she peered out until she could no longer see it. "It is listing very far to one side."

"Yes, the carriage wheel has been removed and was loaded along with your trunks," Ayles assured her.

"So, it will be repaired, and I'll be on my way," she said brightly, hoping there was a chance to not spend a single night under any scoundrel's roof.

"Tomorrow, if the weather lets up," he murmured, picking up his book and spectacles. "You'll have to spend tonight at my estate. I couldn't in good conscience allow your men back to that carriage in the dark and biting cold. The conditions for travel will only get more dangerous by morning, too."

It was fair that he considered the welfare of her servants and the dangers of the road, and she was glad their comfort was uppermost in his mind. But that still left Yvette and her maid alone with a scoundrel.

He glanced her way finally. "Never fear, I won't waste my time chasing you all over the house like Middleton would have done."

She looked across at Ayles, surprised by his promise. She'd been afraid of that, honestly, but he seemed to have an uncanny knack of reading her mind. "Thank you."

He suddenly scowled. "Under the circumstances, it might have been prudent to have waited for your brother instead of storming off in a fit of temper. Not that I blame you for being vexed with him. Rhys has forever been the most unreliable of men. He'll be worried about you."

She clenched her hands under the blankets. "I'd be surprised if he even noticed or cared I wasn't around."

Ayles winced. "He is the worst chaperone in the world, I agree, but he cares about you, too."

"He only cares about himself."

There was sympathy in his gaze, and Yvette couldn't bear to see it. She dropped his gaze, pulled her blanket tight around her, and fought not to cry.

Mr. Ayles sighed. "Your brother knows you've left. I left a note behind to say I saw you leave."

"For Bath," she pointed out. "You yelled at the coachman that this was not the right road. He won't find me, but I'm curious to know how *you* knew I was headed this way?"

"I didn't." He pulled a sour face. "I left right after you, and it's only by chance that our paths have crossed."

Yvette wrung her hands under the blanket. Chance or a disaster. Only time would tell. "It was good of you to leave a note for my brother."

His lips twitched with a hint of a smile. "Not so much of a scoundrel for that, am I?"

She scowled at him, suspicious of his smile. "The day is still young, sir."

He laughed. "Rest easy, Miss Valiant. It's much too cold to seduce anyone."

Yvette was suspicious of his claim but snugged back under the heavy blankets, close to her maid, and kept her eyes on Ayles. The man seemed entirely too pleased with himself.

Chapter Four

As daylight succumbed to darkness, Yvette's annoyance at their slow progress was all too apparent, as was her distrust of him. Luc could feel anxiety radiating off her in waves. This was not what he had planned when he'd left the house party because she'd gone. Finding her carriage broken down on the road had filled him with fear. But once assured she was safe, his mind turned to the inevitable consequences.

She was more or less alone with a bachelor in a carriage taking her far from her chaperone, but he still held out hope that Yvette could come through this with her reputation intact.

And he wanted that. He wasn't a heartless bastard. He only ever wanted to talk to her, and now it was up to him to keep her safe, too.

His home loomed, and he had already decided the best thing to do was place her in the capable hands of his grandmother and leave her be as much as possible.

If he was truly a scoundrel, he wouldn't be so concerned for her reputation.

He put away his spectacles as the carriage turned around on the snowy drive. Above, the men commented upon the cold, and he felt bad for them. Yvette could not have known the fierceness of the storm that still darkened the sky above them.

He climbed out of the carriage as soon as it stopped to greet his butler. "I am in need of a word with the lady of the house immediately," he said quietly. Luc's grandmother lived here and managed his household.

"Oi, monsieur," the butler replied. "I shall inform her of your arrival."

Luc opened the carriage door and beckoned Yvette and the maid out. He didn't try to carry Yvette again, but he did catch her elbow. "We need to talk."

She looked so nervous about even that, and he drew her swiftly inside to the slightly warmer hall. "My servants will show you to a guest room shortly. But I would like to share supper with you. Would an hour be sufficient time to prepare yourself?"

"I don't think…"

Would she refuse to sit down to supper with him, even here, just because he was a scoundrel? That annoyed him. "I just rescued you from freezing to death by the side of the road. If I'd not come along…"

She wet her lips. "If you insist."

Luc ground his teeth. "Thank you."

He let her go and watched her sweep up the stairs of his home with her chin stubbornly set. This wasn't how he'd planned to bring her here.

He returned outside to be certain all was in hand with the carriage and men, and then he went back inside, throwing off his greatcoat and hat to the butler as he went. He made arrangements for dinner, then detoured to the library to pour himself a glass of warming port.

Before he saw Yvette again, he had to speak with his grandmother and make sure she would welcome her and understood the gravity of the situation.

Madelyn Bisset, his maternal grandmother, lived a retired life in the country far from the rest of the family. She preferred this estate over his father's, where, until recently, he'd usually spent most of his time, too. He found her in an adjoining small parlor, a room uncomfortably hot. She cried out in excitement when she saw him, raising her arms to embrace him.

Luc wrapped his arms about her tiny body and lifted her bodily out of the chair. "Grand-mère."

"I thought you'd never come home," Madelyn cried in French.

"I'm only late by a week," he answered in English. "And I bring you a visitor, too."

"*Une femme?*"

"A wife? No." Luc set her back down and dropped into the chair beside her. "I came across Miss Yvette Valiant's carriage broken down on the road not far from here."

Madelyn's eyes sparkled. "*The* Yvette Valiant? You are betrothed to her at last?"

"No, Grand-mère. I have not asked for her hand yet."

"But she is here, and you are here," Madelyn said, forcing a blanket she'd knitted over his knees. "What could be simpler when you carry a torch for her?"

He rolled his eyes, annoyed that he'd confided in her on his last visit. "She still does not like me."

"What is there not to like about my favorite grandson," she chided, pinching his cheek as she'd done to him when he was a boy.

"A great many things still," he said as he carefully folded the blanket and set it aside. "My reputation puts me at a disadvantage."

She slapped his arm playfully. "Every woman knows that a man worth having is a man with a scandalous romantic history."

"Not this one," he warned. Grand-mère was an optimist. She saw nothing wrong with men being scoundrels until they married. Then, betraying one's spouse was an unforgivable offense in her eyes. Her disapproval was widely known in his family. She'd not spoken to Luc's father since he'd gotten himself a mistress.

"Be nice," he begged.

"Am I not always the perfect hostess for you?"

"Oui, madame." He gathered up his grandmother's hand and kissed the back of it. "I must go and change for supper."

She held his hand tightly. "Since when do I care how you look, as long as you are here with me."

"Miss Valiant will join us and she'd expect it of me," Luc warned. "I'll be back soon."

Exactly one hour after his arrival, a change of clothes and far too many warming ports later, the soft patter of feet could be heard coming down the main staircase. He rose as those delicate steps approached and faced the open doorway just as Yvette appeared. She was dressed warmly, he was glad to see. "Miss Valiant. How good of you to come."

She dipped him a brief curtsy. "Good evening."

He bowed. "Might I make an introduction?"

Her brow wrinkled before he stepped aside, revealing his tiny grandmother seated behind him. "I have the honor to introduce you to Madame Madelyn Bisset, my maternal grandmother. Grand-mère, this is Miss Yvette Valiant of Bath."

Yvette's eyes widened before she dropped into a deep curtsy, a blush climbing her pale cheeks. "Oh," she squeaked. "A pleasure to meet you, madam."

Grandmother inclined her head regally, studied Yvette and then looked up at him. "Je pensais qu'elle serait comme tous les autres anglais? Aucun sens du style."

"English please, Grand-mère."

Grandmother had been a foreigner in this country for nearly forty years and stubbornly clung to her habits. French was frequently spoken in this house, but not when he had friends staying.

"It's a pleasure to meet such a cunning young lady," she said.

Luc glanced sharply at his grandmother. "I think you mean *pretty*, yes?"

Grandmother smiled tightly. "Yes, she's pretty cunning to entrap my grandson in such a fashion."

Yvette gaped.

Luc closed his eyes briefly. What Grand-mère had said would not help his cause to win Yvette's trust. "She never intended that," he promised, eager to smooth things over. Grand-mère was convinced every young woman he met must want to marry him.

"You traveled together alone, chérie. Now she must reap what she has sown. Honor demands you wed her."

Luc gaped at his grandmother. "What?"

Grand-mère shuffled across the room to Yvette, caught her arm, and studied her face closely. Yvette tried to escape her grip but Grand-mère was a strong woman for all her slight size.

"We will dine together and I will see what else you are made of besides cunning."

Yvette blinked, rendered speechless, and turned to him, appearing frightened by this new development.

Luc had known this might happen. His grandmother was stubborn and as hidebound by the rules of society as Yvette. It would take a lot to turn her off the idea that he'd compromised Yvette by bringing her here without her brother's permission. But it must be done, and soon. "Grandma, there is no need for us to be married."

"Have you changed your mind about wanting a wife?"

"No."

Yvette's face had become pale during their conversation. She looked as if she was facing the guillotine. He squared his shoulders, fighting back the sting of rejection. "Not like this."

Grand-mère only smiled wider when the butler appeared to announce dinner was served. She drew Yvette away toward the dining room. Luc followed a few steps behind. Yvette didn't trust him, and this, forcing her to wed, would not soften her heart to him one little bit.

"You'll sit closest to the fire and keep warm while we dine, chérie," Grand-mère murmured to Yvette before taking a chair at the head of the table, as was her habit. Luc sat to her right, directly opposite Yvette. A span of mahogany separated them and still it felt like an ocean. Her face was pale, and she had a look of panic in her eyes.

But there was nothing he could do to reassure her he'd not agree to wed her under the circumstances while his grandmother lingered.

They dined in perfectly respectable separation, Grand-mère presiding over their misery wearing a smile. She at least chose to speak English for most of it. But her eyes sparked with triumph and not a little delight in the situation they were in.

He should never have told her about his growing feelings for Yvette. She would use his own yearnings to bring a match about unless he stopped her.

Luc addressed Yvette. "I trust you've been made comfortable upstairs."

"Yes, thank you." She lowered her eyes to the table. "The room is lovely."

He nodded, feeling the compliment had been dragged out of her. "I redecorated the whole house for my grandmother before she moved here. I am exceedingly happy with the work done."

She frowned.

Grand-mère clucked her tongue. "The place was stark and cold before. Too English. No dark, intimate corners or drapes to add warmth. My daughter, Luc's mother, claims the former to be fashionable, but she has no sensibility to make a house a home."

"Grand-mère," he warned. "Do not speak ill of Mammon or I will leave the estate again."

Grandmother did not approve of Luc's mother. She'd become too English for her taste. Luc's mother had discarded her French roots, and the language, the moment she'd married an Englishman in order to fit into society better. Luc understood how hard that was. He was often regarded with distrust for his French ancestry, even when he'd been born in England to an English father.

Grand-mère affected a smile. "As you wish."

Yvette glanced at Grand-mère. "It's a very different home from what I imagined he'd live in."

Grand-mère arched a brow. "Did you imagine my grandson lacked taste?"

Yvette winced. "I didn't know you lived here with him, which is very considerate of him."

She looked exceeding uncomfortable, uttering that bit of praise.

Luc toyed with his wineglass, wondering if she'd thought him heartless as well as a scoundrel. "I am fortunate I can afford my own estate. My mother remains at my father's ancestral home," he shrugged, "but this estate is my favorite, for obvious reasons." He reached for his grandmother's hand and squeezed her fingers. He'd bought this place for himself and for Grand-mère, so they might live in peace away from the stress of family life. His mother and grandmother fought constantly.

"This is why he is my favorite grandchild," Grandmother murmured. "Mon propre fils ignore sa mère."

"She complains that my mother and my aunts ignore her," he explained to Yvette, and then turned on his grandmother. "Grand-mère, you are being rude to Miss Valiant to speak in French. She does not understand you."

Yvette's frown deepened and then she took a deep breath. "I've never met your family apart from Charlotte and her mother."

"Be glad that you have not," he murmured. At her frown, he added, "Mama is ambitious, a shameless flirt, too. My father indifferent to her amors. My parents' rows are not the sort of thing you stuck around to hear at the end of."

She gulped, glancing sideways at his grandmother to judge her reaction to his admission.

"We French are expressive with those we love, child. Love and loathing are so often closely intertwined. Emotion is not something to fear, but embrace, so you remain in control of your destiny. My daughters disdain their heritage to their detriment, and I cannot forgive that."

Yvette pushed food around on her plate. "I hated it when my parents fought."

Luc knew that. He'd met Yvette at a much younger age. Seen her hiding behind a door with her hands pressed hard over her ears to block out the sound of her parents tearing their marriage apart. "I'm sure you heard things you wish you hadn't. I did, too. But I had the advantage of being able to leave, being older and born male."

She nodded slowly, biting her lip.

Luc smiled quickly. "We must try not to let their behavior define our future. You are admired by society, Miss Valiant. You don't always need to fear the comparison to your family. There isn't one."

Grand-mère caught his eye. "You have matured in the last year, chérie," she noted with approval in her tone.

Luc smiled into his napkin and set it aside, since no one seemed to be eating anymore. "May I escort you both to the drawing room for tea?"

"No, I shall retire early tonight." Grand-mère signaled for a servant. "These old bones of mine ache with the cold. You may escort your bride to the drawing room and see to her amusement in my absence."

Luc groaned at the way Yvette stiffened at Grandmother's suggestion. A more skittish woman he'd never met, but they did need to talk. If only to offer her the reassurance she needed.

Yvette stood as Luc's grandmother shuffled from the room, her pace painfully slow.

Luc shook his head. "Two hundred pounds on an invalid chair she needs to get about, and she still won't use it in front of visitors," Luc muttered as her steps faded away.

"A chair might make her feel her years," Yvette suggested in a whisper.

He nodded. "I'm sure you have the right of it. But I don't like to see her struggle."

He turned his gaze on Yvette. She seemed more nervous now they were alone and wouldn't hold his gaze.

"Can you convince her not to force us into a marriage?" she whispered.

"I will," he promised, raking his hand through his hair. "I apologize for Grand-mère, but she is very set in her ways. She's worried about me being alone for some time."

She finally met his gaze. "I've never heard you speak French before."

"It offends many in society given the trouble with France, so I try to sound as English as I can, except around her." He shrugged. "My grand-mother raised me. My parents were occupied with their own affairs, much like yours, I have gathered."

Yvette nodded and twined her fingers together at her waist. "What happens now?"

Luc sat back down at the dining table before he answered. "We get your carriage repaired and you on your way home."

"What about your grandmother? And my brother, and—"

Luc held up his hands to silence the panicked outpouring of words. "There's no sense worrying about all that tonight, Miss Valiant. I'll speak with her again tomorrow and then we'll leave for Bath."

"Traveling together?" Her eyes widened in shock. "Won't that create a bigger scandal?"

"Me, in my carriage, following you in your repaired one," he explained. "I cannot in good conscience allow you to travel so far alone in inclement weather. What if you became stuck again?"

She shuddered. "There is that worry, but... haven't you promised to be with your grandmother for the holiday?"

"She'll accept why I must go with you," he assured her. Grand-mère would not be happy that he had to go, but what could he do. Yvette needed his protection. He tipped his head toward the door. "Don't let me keep you from your bed. We've a long way to go tomorrow to get you safely home to Bath."

Startled by his curt dismissal, she curtsied awkwardly. "Yes, well, good night then, Mr. Ayles."

He nodded. "Sweet dreams, Miss Valiant."

"Yes, and you, too." She started for the door, but turned back to frown at him before she reached it.

He grinned widely, causing Yvette to suddenly trip over her own feet.

He cried out her given name, but she righted herself and scurried away.

He watched the empty doorway for several seconds, then reached for his wineglass. He'd likely have to wait until next season to prove he was a scoundrel she could trust.

Chapter Five

Yvette smoothed her fingers across her brow, determined to rid herself of the stubborn frown line that wouldn't seem to go away that morning. Giving up, she put her head into her hand and grumbled unhappily—very quietly, so no one passing her door might hear.

She had misplaced something. It wasn't something she had ever really liked, but something she had expected to always be around.

Sometime yesterday, she had *lost* a scoundrel.

And it was a worrying thing to discover she might actually miss the disgraceful version of Luc Ayles, too.

For last night, he'd seemed safe.

Protective, excellent company at dinner, affectionate toward his tiny French grandmother. He was everything a good man was supposed to be. He was even prepared to escort her home to Bath at the expense of his grandmother's happiness, too, and that made her uncomfortable.

And when he'd spoken in French, her knees had become decidedly weak, and Yvette did not swoon over *any* man's utterings. She'd known of his heritage, of course, but she'd never heard those sensual tones tumble so effortlessly from his wicked lips.

She'd been affected in the worst way imaginable, afraid he'd notice her discomfort at any moment.

It was startling to realize that since the moment he'd rescued her, she'd hung on his every word.

She went to the window to look at the unceasing white landscape outside. It had continued to snow during the night, and she feared she would be stuck again before half a mile had been traveled. But it was imperative she get away from Luc. She did not trust him, and now she didn't even know *whether* to trust herself.

She let the curtain fall and turned to survey the pretty chamber she'd spent the night in. There were no disgraceful paintings on the walls, and this was no decadent house of sin belonging to a terrible scoundrel.

The place was very properly run, in fact. The maids were polite, respectful and spoke only French, it seemed. Her own maid had reported the servants' hall was a very happy place, too. Everyone here admired Luc.

It was a home any woman would be proud to come to upon her marriage.

She would be proud to live here, but perhaps not with his disapproving grandmother, who insisted they must marry. The old woman had been frosty when they'd met and had lulled her with good company at dinner. But then she'd spoiled her good feeling by reminding her that she and Luc must marry.

Luc had been adamant they not wed, which was both comforting and extremely lowering. He could certainly do worse than become her husband.

Yvette threw herself into a chair close to the fire.

Yesterday, last night, she had feared to be seduced. Or to have fended off a pair of scoundrel's hands by the time she reached the safety of her bedchamber. She had assumed, given all the occasions that Luc Ayles had stared at her with the gaze of a hungry scoundrel, that he had been interested in seducing her. It was decidedly uncomfortable to wake at dawn and feel depressed that he hadn't even tried to find an excuse to seek her out during the night.

Why didn't he at least try

She was an attractive, well-formed lady. Any man should itch to get his hands on her person. She'd enough proof that she appealed to scoundrels, given the number of times she'd avoided them at the house party they'd both left early.

She'd have thought Luc would have stayed longer at the party. He'd no shortage of admirers there.

She glanced toward the locked doorway and then shook her head. "He should want me."

She snatched up her thickest shawl, then threw on her warmest coat, too. Preparing for their next encounter. The scoundrel was sure to reappear soon, and she'd be at ease again, knowing how to respond.

She marched to the door, determined to put herself in his path deliberately and prove him unchanged, but then froze with her hand outstretched.

"What am I doing? This is not who I am."

She did not give scoundrels a second chance. She took a step back, then another. Did she really want to give Luc Ayles a second chance?

Her pulse sped up a bit as an answer became clear. "Heaven help me, but I do," she whispered. "At least he should try to steal a kiss from me one more time."

And there was nothing more shocking to her than the knowledge that she wanted him to try. Was she losing her mind?

She had been good for so long, repressing any and all reckless impulses for fun or misbehavior so she could make a good match. And now, after putting herself in harm's way, being rescued by a scoundrel, and not being even considered for seduction, she was incensed Luc Ayles didn't live up to her expectations.

"And his grandmother expects us to *marry* to avoid a *scandal*," she complained to herself. "There is no scandal!"

Yvette dragged in a deep breath and let it out

slowly. She was working herself up into a state over nothing. She ought to be happy he was minding his manners.

She marched back to the door and threw it open. The hall was empty, but a door along the hall stood open when it had been closed the night before. She became curious and headed toward it.

She tiptoed to the door and risked a peek inside.

Luc Ayles stood at the windows, coatless, his hands on his lean hips. She had never seen him so casually attired, but then again, she'd never peeked into a scoundrel's bedchamber before. But it was as ordinary as hers at home. Quite mundane, really. There was a wide curtained bed, standing looking glass, and trinkets on the mantle.

Her eyes returned to his bed. It was even made up neatly already.

"More snow," he muttered. "*Devil take it!*"

He sounded so angry about the snow that Yvette leaned against the doorframe and sighed her frustration, too. "It's been snowing since I woke at dawn."

He pivoted slowly, eyes wide, to see her standing at his door. "But you *are* ready to leave?"

She nodded to him. "Were your men able to repair the carriage?"

"They've not returned to tell me so yet. I

can't imagine they'll be much longer. We should be underway inside an hour after that."

Ayles suddenly noticed he wasn't properly dressed yet, and he hurried to scoop up his coat and toss it on his rather impressive frame.

How odd that she'd never noticed his physical appeal before, but now, she could almost look her fill without feeling embarrassment.

His expressive eyes met hers suddenly and made her knees tremble again as his long legs carried him to stop right in front of her. He was perhaps the best looking of all scoundrels haunting London's finest homes, and Yvette was all alone with him on his lovely estate.

Almost alone. There was still his grandmother to contend with.

And servants who always gossiped.

And because of her annoyance over her brother's tardiness yesterday morning, she'd put her freedom in jeopardy. They might end up married to each other still.

How *stupid* she was to have engineered a situation that compromised herself. Unwittingly trapping Luc into a situation where honor demanded they wed.

Many women in want of a husband would have rejoiced upon hearing her predicament.

Yvette might have cried about it yesterday.

But not today. Being forced to marry Luc did not seem all that bad this morning. But it was not that good, either. She didn't know very much about him, really.

She wet her lips, and a sense of purpose filled her. If they had to wed, well, something had to be done about that scoundrel side of him. "Well, perhaps they'll return during breakfast."

He looked away to the window. "I hope so. Don't let me keep you."

She was crushed by his dismissal. "Have you already eaten?"

"No."

She smiled tightly. "Then we can eat together."

Yvette held onto her smile as he stepped closer. He was so overwhelming, especially when he was towering over her like this. Yet he inched past her, making sure not to touch any part of his body to hers.

She found his restraint impossible. What would it take for the scoundrel to come back?

He stopped in the hall and raked his hand through his hair. "I'll go ask if the men are back."

"Let's go together," she said, marching toward him so he couldn't escape.

It was hard not to notice he stumbled back a step as she advanced. Was he afraid to be near her because he might have to marry her? She smiled at that. Never had she thought she'd have any power over a scoundrel, and certainly not him.

He had tortured her all season, loitered in

her shadow many a night. She'd give him some of his own back and more, she decided.

At the top of the stairs, she made the mistake of looking down at the steep pitch and suddenly felt dizzy. She blindly extended her hand to Luc.

His fingers captured hers firmly, and he placed her hand on his sleeve and held it there under his warm palm. "Steady. You won't really fall and we're not that high up."

She looked up at him slowly...and blushed that he must already know her secret embarrassment. She'd suffered bouts of dreadful dizziness all her life, though she'd tried to hide it from everyone, including her brother. She felt foolish and self-conscious about her bouts of *wobbles*. Such an affliction often endangered her poise in society.

But somehow, he knew.

She grimaced. "It matters not if the height is one yard or three floors."

"Then hold on to me and the rail until the sensation passes," he murmured.

They descended the stairs together and at the bottom, she breathed a sigh of relief that the horrid descent was over. "How long have you known?"

"I don't know that I've ever *not* known." He frowned. "You always hold tight to any banister or to your brother's arm if he's around. You never stand close to an edge of a balcony, and most women lean forward at the theater to wave at friends in nearby boxes. But you never do."

"Please don't tell anyone," Yvette whispered.

"Why would I do that?"

She glanced up at him. "It's a malady that I'm ashamed of."

He frowned at her. "There is no need to feel ashamed. Lady Crawley faints at the sight of blood and Lady Nells swoons at the sight of the ocean. Even in paintings."

She removed her hand from his arm. He was making fun of her by making up stories about other well-poised women. "You once carried Lady Nells from a ballroom," she complained.

"Yes, our host had hung a new painting and after one glance at it, Nelly fainted, luckily into my arms. Poor thing needed a sherry or two to revive her spirits but couldn't bear to return to the ballroom to view the painting again. I saw her safely home."

"Yes, I heard of that, too," she said slowly, remembering the unsavory gossip after that night. It had been all anyone had talked about for months, entirely salacious, though others thought it wildly romantic, too.

Luc winced.

She shook her head. She shouldn't bring up his behavior, but… "I also heard there was a romantic entanglement between you both."

Luc looked away. "There was. But no more."

And now he was a scoundrel again. Lady Nells had a husband, and children, too.

She walked away from him. Scoundrels, by definition, were not good men. She ought not be surprised to hear the gossip confirmed by his own lips, not that she liked either version.

"I promised you a breakfast before we go," Luc muttered.

Yvette started for the dining room. "Yes."

"We eat in the morning room," he called to her. "It's warmer there."

She spun about and followed him.

But to her chagrin, her gaze drifted from his head to his feet and back up again. He was wicked to have turned her head. It was too bad he was a scoundrel to the bone.

They entered the morning room together and found his grandmother at the table already, sipping tea.

"I will serve myself," she murmured quickly, keen for the distraction of a simple everyday task to restore order to her thoughts.

Luc went to his grandmother. "Grand-mère, Yvette and I will leave soon."

The older woman glared at Luc and turned a spiteful gaze on Yvette. "Why come, if only you will go?"

"Now don't be churlish, ma petite. I promise to return as soon as I see Yvette safely home to Bath. When I return, I'll spend another month with you to make up for leaving you today."

"It will be a cold Christmas this year," the old lady complained

Yvette wanted to sink through the floor. The old woman shouldn't be without her family at Christmas.

Yvette would be alone for much of Christmas this year, too. Her papa was dead, her mother was still on the continent with her lover no doubt, and her brother would likely make some excuse to leave early or not come at all after all this. She slid into a chair, keeping her gaze on her plate, listening as Luc pleaded with the old lady to understand. He spoke softly in French, and with each word and phrase of endearment, she felt worse.

He was leaving because of her.

As she looked around the chamber, she realized the lack of holiday decoration seemed to encompass the whole house. There was no Christmas cheer anywhere in the drawing room or dining room, either, last night, now she thought about it. Had the old lady been waiting for Luc to come to make Christmas and the holiday special?

A tap came at the door and a servant of some kind appeared, cap in hand. "Begging your pardon for the interruption, sir, but you wanted to know about the condition of the road. It's bad. I wouldn't recommend travel in this weather if you can help it."

"What of the carriage and the repair being done?"

"No sign of their return yet. I'm on my way there now to find out what's keeping them. But I thought you should know about the condition of the roads immediately."

She couldn't miss the soft curse that fell from Luc's lips before he dismissed the coachman, imploring him to prepare his carriage still.

A worried expression spread over the old lady's face.

Luc turned to her, his expression grim.

"It sounds dangerous," she murmured.

He nodded. "We'll manage, Miss Valiant."

"No. We'll stay," she decided.

He folded his arms over his chest and stared at her a long time. But then a smile twitched his lips, and he turned to his grandmother. "Looks like we will remain, Grand-mère."

The old lady threw up her hands and beamed with happiness.

Yvette watched her celebrate, not trusting her tongue to express the unexpected surge of relief she felt to have made her decision and have Luc agree.

She shouldn't want to stay in a scoundrel's home, but nor had she been keen to travel in bad weather. And it made Grand-mère happy, too.

Chapter Six

"What do you mean the damn carriage couldn't be repaired because it was gone?"

"I'm sorry to only give you bad news, monsieur," the groom apologized profusely. "The carriage appears to have been taken in the night by thieves. We have searched and searched to no avail."

Luc exhaled his exasperation and slipped the shivering fellow a glass of port to warm his insides. "Not your fault."

The broken-down conveyance had been hacked to pieces overnight. His men had found only splinters in the snow to prove it had been there once.

Rhys was not going to be happy to lose his carriage, even if it was old and in need of replacing. Luc closed his eyes. No doubt the pieces of the carriage were burning in some poor man's hearth, keeping a family warm in this dreadful cold.

A feminine throat cleared behind him. *Yvette*. Catching him unawares again.

Luc turned slowly to face her hovering in the doorway to his study, wearing a warm coat, scarf and woolen gloves.

She shrugged. "I heard what happened, and I had feared as much actually."

He winced. "There is still my carriage for you to take, and my grandmother owns a small curricle. I could travel in that on the way to Bath."

She frowned at him. "The weather is not improving though, and a curricle will be none too comfortable for a long journey."

He swung away to glare out the window. Flurries of snow seemed to be thickening. "It's the only way."

"But the roads are bad and it's not safe to travel today," she reminded him. Yvette was silent behind him a long moment. "We'd best make the most of the time while we can."

He sighed. "How do you imagine we do that?"

"You should spend time with your grandmother while I decorate the house for Christmas. If you'll allow me, that is."

He leaned back against the window frame, puzzled by her lack of distress at their worsening situation. One night might be overlooked. Two? The longer Yvette was here without her brother, the more likely Rhys would imagine the worst. Rhys knew he was a scoundrel. They were cut from the same cloth. "Ah, yes. Christmas." The worst Christmas of her life, no doubt. He admired her plan to decorate his home as a distraction, even if he doubted it would make her happy in the end.

He pushed away from the door and stopped close to her. "I'll have men fetch a Yule log, and greens for the mantle."

He didn't mention mistletoe. He might once have tried to steal a kiss from Yvette under a strategically placed sprig and blamed tradition for it.

She smiled up at him. "It wouldn't be Christmas without them, but I want to go out myself to pick what I need. There's plenty of time now."

"Then I shall have to brave the cold with you," he informed her, expecting to be rebuffed. "Can't risk you taking a wrong road again."

She smiled. "I would appreciate your company."

He smiled carefully lest she change her mind. "It's usually my task to fetch the Yule log and other things. Grand-mère chided me for my tardiness on our arrival."

"You shouldn't have kept your grandmother waiting for you," she said softly. "You don't know how lucky you are to have someone in your family who cares."

"Oh, I know. Grand-mère likes to remind me of it constantly," he replied.

Yvette laughed at that.

Luc's late arrival was entirely because Yvette was being taken to a house party filled with scoundrels. Luc hadn't trusted her brother to act as a proper chaperone in such a venue, and he'd ensured his own invitation to watch over her. A task he didn't mind at all. "There was something I needed to do first. Besides, it's turned out to your advantage to have me be so tardy."

"And I am grateful not to have frozen in my carriage, I assure you."

He smiled and held out his arm. "Shall we brave the cold together now?"

She wrapped her arm about his. "I would like that."

Luc escorted her out to the hall, found a second scarf to wrap about her slender neck. He also caught up a blanket to put around her shoulders for the short walk to the stables. He glanced down at her feet to check she wore sturdy boots. He probably shouldn't carry her in his arms again. That had felt too intimate the first time. "There'll be a good fire burning in the stables once we get there. You can huddle about it while I have a sled prepared."

She turned to him. "A sled?"

He winced and put his hands behind his back. "I promise to behave."

Luc hurried her out to the stables before she could argue that scoundrels didn't know how to behave, and once there harried his men to be quick in getting their sled ready.

Yvette stood by the fire, hands held out, watching him with an inscrutable expression on her face the whole time.

He arranged for his men to follow after them

to cut the log he chose. He then had the very great pleasure of wrapping Yvette in warm furs on the cozy seat inside the sled.

He jumped in beside her, throwing a blanket over his knees, too. "Ready?"

"As I can ever be," she promised with a wry smile.

He pulled the second scarf up over her nose, leaving only her bright blue eyes to admire. "We'll be as quick as we can."

He signaled for a groom to open the stable doors and snapped the reins to spur his horse out into the cold.

Beside him, Yvette put her gloved hands up to cover her eyes. "Ooh, that is chilly."

He winced. "Turn your face toward my shoulder. You'll stay warmer that way."

She glanced up at him, eyes narrowing with suspicion.

He laughed softly. "It's much too cold to act like a scoundrel today, Miss Valiant. Besides, I need both hands for the reins."

The frown returned, but she shuffled closer until her knees pressed against his thigh and she could hide her face in his coat. She twisted a bit more and lay her cheek against his arm to view their passage from the manor house. Beneath the covers, her hands fluttered against his side, but all too soon pulled away. "This is warmer," she called.

"I'm glad," he promised, pulling at his cravat

to cool himself. The pressure of Yvette cuddled against him for warmth made him long for a more intimate setting and far less clothes between them.

Luc pushed the horse to greater speed. Yvette naked was something he shouldn't think about when she was this close. She could always tell when his thoughts turned amorous.

They cleared the paddocks nearest the manor house, and he headed toward the dense woodland. He slowed at the edge of the forest and then stopped in a sheltered spot.

Yvette bolted upright to look around.

Luc stepped out of the sled and tethered the horse to a nearby tree, glad to put a little distance between them. "It's warmer here. Sheltered from the breeze and the worst of the snow."

Yvette fought her way free of all the blankets he'd piled over her. "Oh, this is so charming," she said, looking around with obvious excitement. "Are these woods all yours?"

"As far as the eye can see," he promised. "It's beautiful in the spring, too."

"Oh, I should love to see it then." Yvette jumped from the carriage and ran off into the woods, gloved fingers sliding over the bark of every tree she passed. He'd never taken her for a wood nymph or someone who enjoyed the outdoors before. He smiled and trailed behind everywhere she went, all the while looking for a likely candidate for the Yule log. Grand-mère had a marked preference for size. He'd tie a red-colored rag to the log he wanted cut and his men would find it and cart it back to the manor house by nightfall.

He found their Yule log, marked it and the path to find it, and then he turned to Yvette. Her arms were overflowing with greenery. But she looked so happy, he was momentarily taken aback. It was as if she was enjoying her Christmas with him.

"Here, let me carry all that," he offered quickly, striding toward her to take her burden.

"You don't mind?"

"Of course not. I'll have you know scoundrels are good for more than just carrying women about," he teased.

"I'll have to remember that," Yvette promised.

He took all the greenery from her and looked over each piece. He noted she'd picked no mistletoe today, although there some growing not too far away. Given she seemed to be in charity with him for once, *he* wasn't going to suggest they pick some to hang about a scoundrel's home.

She dithered a bit beside more greenery, arranging pieces unnecessarily in his opinion.

He caught her eye. "We can always come back to the woods tomorrow morning."

"I think there is enough for most of the display but," she stated, "remember this spot, will you?"

"Of course." It was right beside the mistletoe he wished he could pick so he could steal a kiss from her.

He cut a few more branches of holly when she lingered over them and trudged back toward the sled with it all. The horse stamped his feet, impatient to return to the warmth of his stable. Luc went to its head and gave it a rub between its eyes. "You'll be back in the stables soon, I promise."

The horse snorted.

"I don't think he believes you," Yvette taunted.

"Scoundrels are a frequently misunderstood breed," he replied with a careless shrug.

She frowned at him. "Do you *care* what women think of you?"

"I care what *you* think of me."

"You're a good grandson," she admitted after a moment, but she blushed.

He took a step in her direction. "What else might I be?"

"I don't..." She looked up at him. "You're dangerous."

"Not to you. Not if you'd rather me behave."

"I. I don't..." Her brow furrowed. "I think you should be yourself."

His breath whooshed out of him. "Myself. A scoundrel?"

"We'll, scoundrel-ish. It confuses me when you behave any other way."

He laughed at that. "Then I shall be myself and a scoundrel always around you. Try not to slap me as hard as last time, should I attempt to steal another kiss one day."

"I wouldn't do that again. You caught me by surprise and my reaction was ill-considered."

"Ill-considered?" he asked, honestly puzzled. "I deserved that slap for forgetting we might be seen, and you embarrassed."

"No one noticed what you attempted, and the sound of the slap thankfully never drew attention to us."

He nodded. "I can understand why you wouldn't have wanted that. We would have been forced to wed even before you had a season."

"Instead of now," she said, looking away, wincing.

"She will say nothing," he assured her again. "Are you done yet?"

"Almost." She dumped her new gathering of greens into the back of the sled and then straightened.

She was holding mistletoe in her hand.

Luc took a pace back in shock.

Her eyes suddenly widened before she dropped the mistletoe and quickly clambered into the sled, burying herself under the blankets. "I'm sorry," she mumbled.

Luc bent to scoop up the mistletoe and

twirled it around in his fingers as he approached the sled. Clearly, he'd misread the situation. But how could he help but be shocked that she wanted a kiss? He placed the frond in her lap. "This is yours, I believe."

She stared at it. "You don't make me feel worse."

"It's not what you think."

Her jaw set in a mullish line. "I thought you'd jump at the excuse of the mistletoe."

"Mistletoe has long been my excuse for many a wicked deed before," he confirmed.

"I always thought you did whatever you wanted."

"Not anymore."

She stared at him, and it was clear she was confused.

"Am I not—" She did a thing with her hands, her body wriggling on the sled seat, too.

He laughed, and her face reddened.

"Oh, you're impossible."

He strolled around the horse, freed it and turned it about. Then he jumped into the sled beside her. "I know full well you don't like scoundrels trying to kiss you. I won't take advantage of our seclusion here to try."

"But scoundrels don't think about any of that, normally."

He shrugged. "It depends on the woman. Time to head for home, Miss Valiant. My grandmother will be wondering where we are."

He made sure she had covered her up warmly and prepared to drive off.

"Wait." Yvette suddenly grasped his face, gloved fingers capturing his jaw and turning his face to hers. The mistletoe was in her other hand, and it rose above his head. "I'm kissing you, not the other way round."

Her lips were soft and cool against his as she kissed him. Just a peck. A tease, and entirely proper for a mistletoe kiss.

"That was nice," he murmured, expecting nothing more.

"Nice?" Her eyes narrowed on him. "No, that isn't good enough."

And before he could urge the horse to go, she kissed him again.

There was more force behind this kiss, and this time, there was the press of her body against his, too. He hadn't meant to ridicule her kiss or dare her to try again, but apparently Yvette was competitive about certain things. Including kissing him.

Luc couldn't help but respond this time.

Scoundrel he was, and scoundrel he would always be.

Luc pulled her onto his lap, curled his fingers around her skull and showed her what a proper scoundrel's kiss should always entail. He did not hurry. He made love to her mouth with his lips and tongue. He teased his way past the seam of her lips, delving persistently until she was responding with unabashed enthusiasm to every-thing he did.

The brush of her tongue against his made him moan, but he drew back before he went too far with her.

Perched on his lap, Yvette simply stared at him as if she didn't know what to say. He was dangerous to a woman like her, a person determined to live her life free of scandal or passion. It would be best for her if they were never alone again.

Luc lifted her onto the seat at his side, covered her up again and got them underway without looking at her twice. She'd soon realize her mistake and scowl at him.

Chapter Seven

The manor house was ready. Everything was perfect for tomorrow's Christmas Eve feast. She took one last taste of the wassail and then another, making sure the mixture was good enough for Luc.

Warmth crept up her cheeks as she thought of him. He was turning out to be a decent man, and herself a wanton flirt.

Luc now couldn't seem to get far enough from her. Yvette had apparently stumbled upon a way to keep a terrible scoundrel at bay—kiss him first. She should have been happy that he no longer sought her out but instead she felt incredibly sad.

She gave the chamber one last cursory glance, certain nothing more could be done to beautify it for the holiday and then turned for the door. The old woman had asked Yvette to report back to her when she was done with the drawing room.

She crossed the hall to the small parlor the lady of the house used during the day and heard an argument in progress inside. Luc's voice, and the old woman's, were raised and although they spoke only in French, she understood enough to know it was about her being here.

"Do you promise not to make this more difficult than it needs to be?"

"Why should you not have your way?"

"Promise me you will tell Yvette's brother after I've gone that we were never unchaperoned, and especially that he has no reason to doubt Yvette's virtue remains intact. Believe me, she's too innocent to be forced to marry a man like me."

Yvette reared back from the door, shocked by the news that Luc was leaving. She quickly put her ear to the door to learn more.

"I don't know why you won't press your advantage," Madame Bisset grumbled.

Neither did Yvette.

There came the sound of a man frustrated. "Because I love her too damn much to see her unhappily wed to anyone, Grand-mère! Especially me. It doesn't matter that I chose her long ago. She deserves someone much better."

Yvette nearly swooned. Luc loved her? How could that be?

But surely, he would not lie about such an important thing to his grandmother. She put her eye to the crack in the door to see the old lady nod. "If it's what you want, I will do as you say."

"Thank you, chérie," Luc said, sounding relieved. "It's for the best. Excuse me. I need to see to a few things before I go."

With the conversation over and Luc's heavy tread heading toward the door, Yvette beat a hasty retreat to the drawing room across the hall. She went to the fireplace, fiddled with a branch of holly draped across the mantle, but her mind was in a whirl.

Scoundrels didn't declare they loved women to their grandmothers, then planned the next moment to leave them.

And why did he love her?

She plopped down in a chair and put her head in her hand.

Of all the men who had pursued her in the past year, never would she have imagined Luc had any honorable intentions concerning her.

"I hope you're not about to tell me you caught a chill while we were out gathering Christmas greens," Luc said suddenly, surprising her with his question.

Yvette looked up slowly, afraid of frightening him off again. Luc was poised at the doorway, watching her and looking very appealing.

Her heart skipped a beat and she struggled for a response. The man loved her, though that seemed impossible. He wouldn't even try to kiss her when mistletoe had been present. And in recent days, he'd been avoiding her.

His smile faulted. "*Are* you ill?"

"I was thinking," she murmured.

"Looks painful. I assumed the frown was because I've disturbed you again," he said.

Sadly, he was far from the truth. She wasn't sure what to say to him now.

"I apologize for the interruption," he said quickly, wincing.

She stood. "You've no cause to apologize. I have not always been in charity with you, have I?"

"For good reason."

"Well, scoundrels should never apologize," she said, her heart beginning to race. "Won't you join me."

"I have a few things still to do."

Before he left? "Please," she whispered. "I would be glad for your company."

"That must be a first." Luc offered a wry smile. "I am quite aware of your dislike of scoundrels."

She winced. "I don't mind talking with you, Luc."

Luc regarded her with surprise and then he came a single step closer and put his hands behind his back. "How have you been, Miss Valiant?"

"Very well, thank you." She met his gaze. "Have you been avoiding me?"

His expression suggested he had been trying to do just that.

She gaped at him. "But why?"

"You know why."

She gulped.

"You understand, don't you? It's best for your

reputation." He took a step back, clearly intending to leave her alone again.

She cast her eyes about the room, hoping to give him reason to stay a little longer. Luc was turning out to be a completely unique scoundrel. A man she wanted to be near very much. But her palms were damp with nerves. He was handsome and kind and now, very appealing. "What do you think of the room?"

He walked a circuit of the chamber, examining everything she'd done while he'd been avoiding her company. She appreciated his intense scrutiny of her efforts. Her brother barely noticed or commented on the changes she made at home unless he tripped over them.

His gaze returned to hers. Piercing and direct. A habit she had found disconcerting in a crowded ballroom where others might notice the direction of his interest. "Very festive," he assured her. "But then, you do everything well that you try your hand at, I've noticed."

A thrill went through her at his praise though she tried to keep the pleasure of it off her face. Her mother had been shamelessly affected whenever a man paid her a compliment. She'd always thought she was different. "I was just on my way to tell your grandmother that I was done. Will she be pleased, do you think?"

"I would never dare speak for her, but I think she'll be happy simply because she'll have company tomorrow. I suspect you both enjoy the winter holiday in equal measure."

"So will you, I promise," she said quickly. But only if he stayed with them.

Somehow, she and Luc had gravitated toward each other as they'd spoken. She was near enough to reach out and touch him. And he could do the same.

But he didn't.

His hands were behind his back, only his eyes betrayed that spark of keen hunger was still there whenever he looked at her for too long.

She could not forget that Luc had told his grandmother he was in love her, too. It made his intension to leave painful to her. She'd thought him a scoundrel with *all* women. But here he was, alone with her in an intimate setting, and he was again behaving like a gentleman.

Would she always need a sprig of mistletoe to make him remember who he really was before he kissed her?

But there was none in the room.

Luc inched closer. "Thank you for making the holiday so memorable for my grandmother, and for me, too."

She hadn't done very much, not compared to the lengths she went to at home for a brother who cared little for the holiday himself. Preparing for Christmas here in Luc's home had been much more satisfying than she'd ever expected. "You are welcome, and I rather think setting off into a storm is something we'd both be keen to avoid."

"That wasn't the memorable thing." He suddenly slipped his finger under her chin and tilted her face up. "Thank you for kissing a terrible scoundrel."

She met his gaze full of embarrassment for her past behavior. "You're not really the worst."

His finger dropped from her face. "Who is the worst you've dealt with?"

"Middleton has been rather persistent. He keeps trying to steal a kiss from me, no matter how much I fight him off," she complained.

His gaze fell from hers. "Middleton would not offer matrimony should you succumb to his advances. Did you tell your brother about him?"

"I tried, but he only listed the man's assets, as if I only care about material possessions and connections. He thinks it a good match."

"He'd make you miserable with his philandering," Luc warned, his voice low and urgent.

"I know." Luc remained close and she could inhale the scent of his now familiar cologne and imagine his strong arms holding her again. He made her nervous and she turned away in a panic. "Would you care for a glass of wassail?"

Luc wasn't that much of a scoundrel at all, really. Not when compared to Lord Middleton's dogged pursuit. Luc had turned out to be...*nice*.

Warmth began to creep up her cheeks as Luc followed her to the wassail, and her hands shook as she measured out a serving for him and herself.

She passed him a glass but noticed his grim expression.

Yvette clasped her cup tightly. "Is something wrong?"

"Very wrong." He pressed his lips together hard and shook his head. "I am sorry to say that I must leave you. I ought to go fetch your brother and make sure he knows you're safe."

"But you can't leave now," she gestured around her, "everything you must love is here."

"That is true," he murmured.

Yvette buried her nose in her glass, her face flaming with the pleasure of his words, and then because the wassail had been so tasty, she refilled her glass. "You must really try this. Wassail is a specialty of mine."

Luc inhaled the aroma of the contents of his glass, but did not taste it. "Is it now? Well, I should at least taste it once I suppose."

"Yes, you should." She looked up at him and, while she sipped hers, her heart started to beat faster and faster. "My father always used to make a toast at Christmas."

He nodded. "Perhaps you would allow me the honor?"

Yvette nodded. What would a scoundrel toast to?

Luc raised his glass. "To family and friends, great or small wherever they are. In good times and in bad, may their lives be rich with new experiences and their doors always remain open to opportunities."

"And free of snow," Yvette added quickly, sipping from her glass.

Luc laughed and then took a sip. Yvette watched his expression change as the flavors of her wassail reacted with his senses. "Oh my. That *is* different."

"Good different or the other?" she asked, taking another sip from her glass, watching Luc intently as he sampled from his glass again.

"Very good indeed." He'd drained his glass and looked eagerly at the wassail bowl. "So good that I'll need a refill to take with me and demand the recipe."

Yvette preened as he refilled his glass, and she topped up her own again, too. "There's apple cake to share, as well. This one is your grandmother's cook's recipe, I believe."

"An old favorite of my stomach's," he confided.

"I thought you wouldn't care for family traditions," she murmured, quickly downing another bit of her wassail. "You surprise me."

He took a plate with a slice of cake from her. "You've always surprised *me*. I beg you, don't stop now."

That made her smile, and she realized her cheeks were still hot. It could have been from the wassail, but it was most likely because of the scoundrel standing so close again. A scoundrel she'd like to encourage.

Yvette had never flirted with a man in her life. She'd been too afraid of embarrassing herself or causing gossip that might ruin her chance to make a good match.

But that version of herself was slipping away, thanks in part to the wassail and the holiday, and a bolder, more courageous Yvette had taken her place. Her interest in Luc seemed to know no bounds as she sipped her wassail, studying him. She wanted to be the sort of woman he'd want to kiss. But how to give him the right nudge in that direction escaped her.

He finished his cake and set his empty cup down, too. "Well, I'd best go before the servants' tongues start to wag."

If he left now, would she ever feel this bold with him again?

Fearing she might not, Yvette reached out to touch his face before he could make his escape. She let her fingers linger on his warm skin, glad that she wasn't wearing gloves this time. She let her fingertips drag along his jaw, noticing the roughness of stubble against her flesh. She took a moment to enjoy the look of stunned surprise on his face. In her season of searching for a husband, she'd never wanted to touch a man's face before.

"Yvette," he murmured.

"Luc," she whispered back as her eyes were drawn to his mouth.

He pursed them a moment and then whispered, "How much wassail have you consumed today?"

She brushed her curled fingers against the grain of his stubble again. "I had to taste it as it was made. It's important to get the flavors just right. And I've had this glass with you."

"Three glasses, actually," he said. "You topped up your glass more than mine."

Yvette blushed, realizing she'd drunk more than she usually would at home. "Usually, my brother helps with the tasting."

"It shouldn't have been enough to make you forget the proprieties, so I have to ask, what are you doing with my face?"

She frowned as she ran out of stubbled jaw to stroke and dropped her hand. There had been reasons, many good reasons, to ignore Luc's appeal before. But today they all seemed pointless avoidances of a certain uncomfortable truth— she was more attracted to him than she realized.

She would like this Christmas to be memorable for better reasons than just being stranded here.

"I don't really know," she admitted.

A tiny smile curved up his lips. "When you do decide what it is you want from me with a clearer head, come and find me."

"I can't if you still plan to leave to fetch my

brother," she pointed out. She wanted him to stay. She wanted him to kiss her, too.

He leaned close but his lips only lightly grazed her cheek before he headed for the day. "I'll stay...but only because you *want* me to," he said, then promptly disappeared again.

Chapter Eight

It had taken all his strength to back away from Yvette yesterday, but it had been the right thing to do then. He wasn't sure it was Yvette touching him, or a woman bolstered by too much wassail, making her forget all she'd held dear for so long.

But how glorious it had felt to have her fingers drawing lazy circles along his jaw. Not that he supposed she realized what she was doing to him before he'd pointed it out. It probably had been the wassail lowering her inhibitions. Such behavior was completely out of character for her.

If he'd been the scoundrel she expected, she'd have been bedded that very afternoon.

Luc adjusted his cravat one more time and decided he was as ready as he would ever be to face her again. He'd given her plenty of time and space to decide what she'd do next with him. She could pretend yesterday's caresses never happened. He half expected that, honestly. But he had luncheon to sit through, opposite Yvette, and he could not avoid her. If Yvette wasn't ready for a future as a wife, he'd accept that too.

He would see how she reacted to him at luncheon and let her behavior be his guide.

He exited his chambers and headed downstairs. Grand-mère stood on the threshold of the drawing room, back rigid and glaring at Yvette's slumped form beside the fire.

"What is going on?"

"Wake her," she demanded. "This is not the way any woman should sit in my drawing room."

He strolled to her chair, settled a gentle hand on her shoulder and then shook her.

Yvette startled upright, blinking, and he quickly moved away. "I wasn't asleep."

"Of course not," he promised, trying not to grin. The room was stifling hot, which must have contributed to her drowsiness.

A fiery blush was climbing her cheeks now. He went to pour her a glass of water and took it to her. "Here, drink this. It might help clear your head."

She gulped it down, and Luc rejoined his grandmother at the door to give Yvette time to compose herself. "Happy Christmas Eve, chérie," he whispered before kissing her soft, wrinkled cheek.

Grand-mère smiled up at him. "Always a charmer."

"I learned from the best. You," he said and then looked over his shoulder. Yvette seemed more awake now and her blush was fading. "Happy Christmas Eve, Miss Valiant," he called.

"And to you, sir," she said with a shy smile in his direction.

He prowled the room, keeping a watchful eye on Yvette and his grandmother as they exchanged pleasantries. If he was to ever marry Yvette, he needed these two to get alone if he had any chance of a happy home life. "I see the snow has finally stopped falling. If all goes well, we can be on our way the day after tomorrow."

"At least you will be here for Boxing Day now," Grand-mère chided.

He glanced at Yvette, wondering if she missed her home this holiday. She hadn't seemed unhappy spending Christmas here so far, but she hadn't talked about Bath much, either. "We will see what the future holds."

She nodded, too.

It might be too late by then to prevent harmful gossip about Yvette. The more days she was with him, the more certain Luc was that her brother would arrive, cross. Rhys would assume the worst. He only hoped he did not punish Yvette too harshly. He hoped Rhys would not force them to wed.

"Will anyone come calling today?" Yvette was asking.

"No," Grand-mère informed her.

Luc rushed to explain when his grandmother didn't try. "My grandmother has never wanted the tenants to brave the evening winter weather. Most likely some of the closest will come tomorrow morning if the weather holds fair, and I will go out sledding alone to see the aged and farthest tenants on Boxing Day."

Her face fell, clearly disappointed by the news they'd have so little company calling on them. "In Bath, we often have had callers until midnight on Christmas Eve and all of Christmas Day. It's a very jolly time, taking turns to call on our friends' homes there."

He smiled. "It must be fun, indeed. But unfortunately, you must make do with our company. I wouldn't want anyone I know getting lost or stranded on a snowy afternoon."

"No," she agreed with a quick smile for him. "That isn't at all pleasant."

Luc winked at Yvette. "But even if we cannot have a houseful of visitors, we have the promise of a beautifully decorated home, a great feast ahead of us, and my grandmother is sure to regale us with stories from her childhood in France if we ask her nicely."

He grinned at his grandmother, and she scowled. "My stories are for family."

He took up his grandmother's hands and kissed them. "But you will make an exception for Miss Valiant, who is without her brother and friends this holiday, yes?"

Grandmother nodded. "As you wish, ma petite."

Yvette frowned. "What is that she calls you? Is it a nickname?"

Luc laughed softly. "I was hoping you

wouldn't notice. Ma petite means little. An ill-suited endearment for a fully grown man that she will not cease uttering, no matter how much I beg and plead for her to stop."

"If you marry Yvette, I will stop," Grand-mère promised with a sweet accompanying smile.

"Hmm," he mused, then noticed Yvette's smile had slipped. "She loves to tease." Luc noticed the butler waiting at the door and was glad for the distraction. "Ah, looks like luncheon is served. I hope you are both starving."

Usually, Luc wasn't so enamored of Christmas in the country with his grandmother. But Yvette was here, and it seemed different because of her presence. Happier. His heart merry and suddenly full of optimism.

The table nearly groaned under the weight of all the food. There was so much laid out that there was barely any room for their place settings. Dozens of candles illuminated the table and the room, and combined with Yvette's decoration, it had created a bright, warm atmosphere. Just as Grandmother always wanted.

He smiled at Yvette—then gasped.

Tears were streaming down her cheeks. "It's all so beautiful," she whispered. "So beautiful."

Luc reached inside his coat pocket and offered her the linen to dry her eyes with. "It's going to be a wonderful Christmas."

She sniffed and wiped her eyes. "I haven't

had a holiday feast like this since my father passed away. He loved the holiday and feasts. I could never quite capture the spirit of the season when I was the only one who cared."

Grand-mère patted Yvette's arm, muttering soothing promises in French that she was always welcome with them. Not that Yvette could understand a word she said. However, the tone of Grand-mère's voice must have been soothing enough to do the trick, because Yvette nodded and forced a smile. She wiped away her tears and put her sadness away soon after.

Luc went to his grandmother to drop a kiss to her hair. "Thank you for cheering her up."

"I see now why you like her so much," Grand-mère whispered in French. "She's nothing like your other women. She believes in family and tradition, too. She would have made an admirable wife for you."

Luc, forever grateful Yvette understood nothing of French, said nothing in response. He helped the ladies to their places and picked up a set of serving spoons.

"It is our tradition that my grandson serves us," Grand-mère murmured to Yvette. "It is our turn to be spoiled."

He nodded. "Do you mind very much, Miss Valiant? In my family, it is the duty of the youngest man present to serve on Christmas Eve."

"Not at all," she promised. "Please proceed."

Luc moved around the table, serving his grandmother a selection from every platter or bowl. When it came to Yvette's turn, he gave her tiny portions of everything.

Yvette murmured her thanks, but now Grandmother was frowning.

"You forgot to give her goose, Luc," Grandmother chided.

"Miss Valiant dislikes it," he murmured, as he sat down to serve himself last. "On account of her father's manner of death."

"I'm sure it tastes delicious." Yvette looked at him curiously. "I've never told anyone about my avoidance of goose."

He'd not needed to be told. He'd been watching Yvette all season. They had a lot of mutual acquaintances. "A servant plonked a piece on your plate at Horsham's dinner, and your face became so pale I feared you might faint."

"You *were* paying attention." She beamed a gentle smile at him that almost made him blush. And it made him think of kissing her and doing other dark deeds his grandmother ought not be present for. "You are worth paying attention to," he promised and cleared his throat before making sure the ladies' glasses were filled with wine.

"Thank you for saying that," she whispered.

He nodded and eventually circulated back around the table, replacing empty plates with fresh for the desert course to come.

Yvette's cheeks were pink with a blush still. He was very glad he gave her only half a glass of wine. It wouldn't do to have her under the weather two days in a row.

Grand-mère reached out to pat Yvette's arm. "Are you happy here, chérie?"

"It's not exactly the Christmas you'd hoped for," he said quickly.

"No," Yvette agreed, her gaze flicking to his and holding it a second too long before she looked down. "But I have everything I need and more. Thank you for making me so welcome."

Luc sat back and her eyes returned to his, again holding his gaze longer than normal.

Now what is that look about?

He served the dessert course. Yvette's color was still high, and her breath came a little faster than normal. Did he dare hope she really was softening toward him at last? Even without wassail?

The devil inside him rejoiced, but he wanted to be sure. To test her interest, he cautiously extended his leg under the table until he brushed her skirts. Then he lifted his foot higher, brushing up the outside of her calf with his toe and back down to her ankle.

She startled but in no other way betrayed to his grandmother what he was up to under the table.

He started up her leg again, and a tiny smile turned up the corners of her mouth before she stifled a laugh. She pretended it was a cough and then filled her mouth with the excellent trifle that completed their feast. He kept moving his foot against her and the tiny smile on her lips remained.

Eventually, he withdrew his leg and she looked across at him. He saw the exact moment she accepted and missed his advances. The softening of her expression, the relaxation of her body, a slight pout that she couldn't have more. There was unabashed interest in her eyes when she held his stare. He knew women...but he'd never seen Yvette like this.

Luc's pulse raced. Anticipation and desire tightened every muscle in his body.

He'd won her acceptance of his nature—but could he win the rest of her, too? He needed her heart as well as her delightful body in his bed for the rest of his life.

They lingered at the table, Grand-mère regaling them with stories from her past. Yvette seemed happier. She laughed along with him and kept glancing his was. Occasionally, he reached out to her under the table to reminder her he'd not lost interest. He was painfully aware that the woman he'd wanted for so long sat just a few feet away, allowing him to touch her. But there was only so far he'd go in a seduction in front of a witness. He needed to be alone with Yvette again and ask if she'd let him pursue her.

Chapter Nine

Christmas Eve had been a great success. Yvette hadn't enjoyed herself so well for a long time. It had felt like she'd been with family again. Grand-mère told such fascinating stories of a life lived elsewhere. And Luc...well, he was again the wicked scoundrel she'd always taken him for, touching her leg under the dining table and pretending innocence. She didn't know how he managed it. It had taken all her strength to keep a straight face and not give away what he was doing. That would only convince his grandmother that something was going on between them.

And when he stopped, and then started up again, she found it hadn't been unwanted attention. He was far more practiced at flirting than she'd ever be, and he was very good at it. He had more experience than her, and with other women, too.

A sourness filled her stomach as she thought of those other women—beautiful, accomplished, wanton, and falling all over him back in London's ballrooms. But he'd not remained involved with any for long. He'd never fallen in love with those wicked ladies. He'd fallen in love with her, Yvette Valiant, a very proper lady.

She was excited by that. Nearly breathless with anticipation for what he'd do next.

Right now, Luc and his grandmother were sitting at the pianoforte playing a duet across the room, him looking devilishly handsome and happy to be at home, his grandmother smiling and teasing him. It was sweet how Luc doted on the older woman. Her own brother had never behaved in such a way with their grandparents. It made Luc the better man in her eyes—even if he *was* the terrible scoundrel she'd believed dangerous to her heart.

He might always be that way, too.

For a change, the idea of Luc being wicked didn't worry her so much as it had before. She'd thought she understood him, but there was more to him than had first met her eye. He flirted as if he was born knowing how to confound a woman's sensibilities, but he was also kind; he'd never forced his attentions on her, and he'd had ample time. And she couldn't forget he had taken the trouble to learn something deeply personal about her feelings and fears.

She detested geese because of the manner of her father's death. No other gentleman, scoundrel or not, had truly bothered learning the first thing about her life before the season had started. They'd only considered her pretty features and the size of her dowry, her brother's indifference, before pouncing on her at every opportunity.

How could Luc ever have loved such a creature as she'd been to him, and so often rebuffed? She'd been cold and dismissive of his interest. Unwilling to give him the time of day.

Was it only a few days ago that she'd feared being alone with him? Now she hoped for another opportunity so she might learn more about this extraordinary scoundrel. She'd like another kiss before Christmas Day arrived, too. She'd liked the feel his strong arms wrapped about her.

She let out a heavy sigh. How did a proper lady express her desire to be only a little wicked with a man of such vast experience as Luc without making a fool of herself? There were few of the traditional opportunities to be close to a man here. There was no dancing and no Charlotte to ask for advice.

The music stopped abruptly. "I hope we're not tiring you, Miss Valiant?"

She blushed seeing Luc so concerned about her. "Not at all. I was wishing that my friend could be here to twirl about the room with to the music."

"You and Charlotte do love to twirl." Luc laughed suddenly and then whispered into his grandmother's ear. He stood up from the pianoforte. "Perhaps you'd allow me to stand in for Charlotte tonight?"

She gaped as he crossed the room in three quick strides, hand extended.

He smiled down, a devilish light in his eyes.

"Might I have the pleasure of a dance, Miss Valiant?"

Yvette looked up into his handsome face and trembled. She saw a longing there she'd never seen before. She always tried to avoid dancing with the scoundrel. She'd given Luc the honor only once before. But tonight…tonight she had no excuses nor desire to refuse him anything, it seemed.

She placed her hand in his and was tugged toward the only open space nearby. The front hall's beautiful parquetry floor gleamed under candlelight, far from his grandmother's view.

Luc spun her about as soon as the music commenced, lifted his hand high above her head so she could duck underneath and return to his embrace. "How did you know about Charlotte and I twirling, Luc?"

"I'm always interested in everything you do, Yvette. You fascinate me," he admitted.

"We only do that where no one should see us," she chided. "Were you following us?"

"Scoundrels are everywhere, Miss Valiant," he warned. "I preferred to know that you and Charlotte were not being bothered by the others too much."

She laughed at that and leaned into his embrace a little more. "Thank you, but you haven't been that successful, I'm afraid."

"I've done more to protect your reputation than your brother has," he promised. "I've even threatened my fair share of scoundrels with dismemberment should any part of their anatomy besides fingertips touch any part of you."

She blushed, wishing for more of Luc to touch her tonight. His fingers spread across her upper back were warm and firm, directing her around the lower floor until the music his grandmother played became almost too faint to hear properly.

She met his gaze with certainty. She wanted him to want her. To flirt with her and care about her. She didn't have a clue how to ask for that, so she just held his gaze and waited.

He slowly raised his fingers to caress her cheek. "You are so lovely, but you should never do with me what feels wrong for you."

"I know."

He pulled her back to his arms and they danced more slowly this time, back into his grandmother's presence. She was twirled around and around until she cried out that she was falling.

Falling in love with a handsome scoundrel, who seemed to love her enough to wait until she was ready to be seduced.

And she was. She gulped and stumbled back to sit on the settee, hands to her flaming cheeks. "I've never been twirled like that before."

Luc winked. "That's just the first of many surprises for you, I hope."

He turned away, returning to play another

tune with his grandmother until she announced it was time for her to retire. Luc swept his grand-mère up in his arms suddenly and, despite her protests, carried her from the room with a promise to return shortly.

Yvette used the time alone to catch her breath and draw on her inner strength to face a difficult decision on what to do about Luc Ayles loving her.

He might seduce her tonight if she gave him any encouragement.

And then what? Would he marry her? He did not seem averse to the notion of being a husband. And hadn't Charlotte said he had chosen someone?

Had he chosen Yvette and hidden that from his cousin?

She turned to him as he strode back into the chamber. He shut the doors behind him, but he went straight to the pianoforte and began to tidy up the music sheets. "She hates to be carried, but it's Christmas Eve and I think I got away with spoiling her."

"You're her favorite grandson. I think you might be forgiven any spoiling," she told him, watching as he left everything just so and then finally turned in her direction.

He grinned. "She *has* punished me before."

"I can hardly believe she'd scold you for any-thing, Luc."

His grin widened. He'd not missed that she'd

used his given name. "I once made a secret wager to race against a neighbor from my front steps to the nearest village. My horse was hardly broken, and though I won, she sent me to my room for a month."

"You could have been killed," she whispered

"Would you have missed me?" he teased.

"If you'd died as a boy, I'd never have known you," she pointed out.

He grinned and came closer. "I would never have known you, either."

He was suddenly sitting by her side. She glanced his way. That look in his eye was back… the one that suggested he was undressing her in his thoughts. She took a deep breath. "Is knowing me so very important to you?"

"The most important thing in my life. For instance, right now, the look you just gave me tells me I'm sitting much too close, and you need space." He shuffled back a bit and stretched out his long legs toward the fire. "I've always wished you were more comfortable around me."

She bit her lip. She wasn't uncomfortable with him anymore. She was simply uncertain of what to do around him, now that she'd started to like him. "I have gotten used to seeing your face."

He brightened with surprise. "Have you been sipping the wassail again?"

She laughed at his teasing. "No. I think I'll

leave tasting the wassail to you and my brother in the future."

"The future," he said slowly. "Yvette, do you think you're as right-minded as you ever can be tonight?"

"Yes. I think so."

"Good, for I have an important question to ask you." He shuffled a little closer on the settee. "Do you think you might miss me when we part ways?"

She nodded. "I will."

He let out a laughing breath. "Will it surprise you to learn I don't want to take you back to Bath because I'd miss you, too?"

Her cheeks heated with a blush. "No. I've come to suspect I've seriously misjudged your interest in me."

He leaned his upper body in her direction to whisper, "I am a scoundrel, my dear. You were right about that. Always."

She scowled at him. "A true scoundrel would have taken advantage of me by now."

He laughed again. "With my grandmother in the house?"

"It's not unheard of. A great many marriages start because a woman was compromised," she reminded him. "My mother tells me—"

Luc groaned and held up his hand for her to stop. "I think the worst thing your mother ever did was confide in you about the *ton's* scandals. It has colored your view of all gentlemen and marriage. Scoundrels can be exciting, and many become good husbands, too. Proper gentlemen with perfect manners tend to be dull conversationalists and utterly boring in bed. I'm not boring in bed," he promised.

A fiery blush climbed her cheeks, and she was frozen in place. Luc waited, watching her… and not pouncing. Waiting for her to decide what might happen between them. She gulped and looked him in the eye.

"Yvette," he whispered. "Do you want that kiss now? Knowing full well I'm a terrible scoundrel and have kissed dozens of other women?"

Her frown returned. "There's no reason to rub in my face you liked them more."

"They were practice, while I was waiting for you to notice me."

"You're hard to miss."

He grinned. "And I've been so very annoying, haven't I?"

"Yes. You were always putting yourself in front of me or shadowing me."

He uttered a helpless sigh. "I'm drawn to you, but I never wanted to ruin you."

She blinked several times and then scowled at him. "I think I could have stopped you before things went too far."

"What now?" He glanced to the window. "Yvette, it started snowing again during dinner. I cannot promise that the roads will be clear tomorrow or the next day. I will take you home if you still wish to go, and we can see each other again next season in London. But it's always been your choice what happens between us." He smiled softly and lowered his head to hers. "What do you want, chérie?"

Chapter Ten

Luc held his breath as he placed fate into her tiny hands. There were men more deserving of her affection, and her hand in marriage.

"I..." She looked up at him, eyes flashing with defiance. "Let it snow, Luc. Let me stay here with you."

Luc grinned, his heart nearly bursting with happiness.

He'd won Yvette. She'd never offer herself to a scoundrel without it meaning forever.

He swooped in to steal a kiss and received an awkward response. Yvette hardly seemed to know what to do with passion, but he'd be patient and teach her his wicked ways soon enough.

He turned toward her, lifting his hand to caress her soft cheek.

Startled eyes met his, and then her gaze fell to his lips.

Luc kissed her again, gently at first, and showed her how proper scoundrels seduced their lovers. Slowly and thoroughly.

Her fingers rose to his hair, her chest pressed to his as he held her in his arms. He drew back to see the face of the woman he loved swept up by the sweetest passion he'd ever known.

She raised drowsy, lust-filled eyes to his and then suddenly scowled.

Luc laughed and attempted to brush away her frown line with his thumb. "You are so lovely, even when you scowl at me."

But she just stared at him. Watching, waiting for what he'd do next.

He smiled and tweaked her nose. "I'd best let you go to bed. We can continue this tomorrow if you like."

And when she was gone from the room, he'd work to calm his body so he could go to his own alone and make plans for them. But currently, his trousers were tented over his groin. He had placed his arm across his lap, determined not to frighten her with the evidence of his state of arousal.

"I'm not tired," she whispered. "And I'm not a child, Luc. I know what you want from me."

"That can wait until you're ready," he promised. "I'll still be wicked tomorrow."

"Luc, you're not hearing me. I don't want to wait until tomorrow. I want to be with you tonight."

He studied her face. Saw uncertainty but also determination. Of its own accord, his hand rose to cup her cheek. "Darling Yvette," he whispered. "I want you more than words can say but you don't realize what that means yet."

She laughed softly. "Is there an instruction book for scoundrels, Luc? A set of instructions for the pace of seductions? If so, please toss it into the fire. You are the most unpredictable scoundrel I've ever encountered."

He grinned that she was showing a playful side, and not to mention more than a little impatience to be seduced. Lovemaking didn't always have to be a serious business but being with Yvette was. He'd love nothing more than to coax her toward his bed with laughter if she was truly ready.

Her hand rose to his face, caressed his jaw, and he sighed at the heaven found in her touch. She released him…and her hand dropped to his cravat. She tightened her fingers on it and pulled him determinedly closer. "Kiss me, scoundrel," she demanded in a whisper.

So, he did.

And it was glorious.

Yvette quickly learned she could kiss him witless and use her tongue, too, all the while striving to plaster herself to his body.

He lay her down upon the settee and moved to cover her body with his.

The first touch of his lower half to hers brought a startled gasp tumbling from her lips. He exerted all the patience he could muster to take things slow until their bodies were intwined and they were both panting.

Luc began to thrust his hips a little against her sex. Knowing pressure there would arouse her, and also prepare her for what could happen between them next. Yvette was a virgin, so he'd be content just to see her climax and deny himself any pleasures until after they married, if that's what was required.

Yvette suddenly gasped and pushed him off her a little. "I know what you're doing to me."

Chest heaving, pulse racing, he cursed his impatience. "I'm sorry."

"Don't apologize." Her frown returned. "Shouldn't we discard our clothes first?"

His cock throbbed at the idea of being so free with her. But it was winter, and the room was not that warm. He should have thought to stoke the fire earlier, but he had not planned for this. "We could but it's not absolutely essential. We could continue wearing our clothes until you cry out in climax. There are more ways to love each other than the obvious ravishment by a scoundrel."

Her fingers teased into his hair. "I like my scoundrel."

He smiled. "Reformed scoundrel now."

"I know your expressions, too, Luc. You want to make love."

"Just to you, no one else." He looked down into her flushed face. She was not so overcome with passion that all her senses were impaired. Yet she knew far too much about illicit affairs for his liking. But that wasn't what this was at all. He had to make it clear. "I don't just want you today, but forever, Yvette."

There. He'd declared himself. All that was needed was to go down on one knee. But he'd do that tomorrow, in a proper setting with his grandmother watching on.

She grinned. "Forever, then."

She drew his face down to be kissed, and Luc's restraint crumbled to dust under her inexperienced assault. He slowly hitched up her skirts to her waist and lowered himself to lie as close as possible. Then Luc turned them onto their sides and grasped her thigh to urge her uppermost leg over his.

Her fingers fumbled at his waist, hesitant, uncertain again before they withdrew.

"Touch me," he gasped. "Hold me."

Yvette's hands returned to his waist, and he gasped at each button of his trousers that she undid. Her touch was light at first but gradually became bolder, sliding beneath his waistcoat and shirt, under the fall of his trousers, too, until finally she touched the bare skin of his lower stomach.

He kissed her parted lips and caught her gaze as he slid his hand to rest directly over her quim. Her hips jerked, and she shuddered. She did not ask him to stop but was biting her lip, worrying it.

"That's it. Get used to me touching your body. I'll take things so slow. I've always dreamed of this moment," he confided in a whisper.

He teased his fingers through her crisp curls

and gently parted her folds, at first finding her dry and unaffected by passion. But as he delved a little deeper, he encountered her damp heat, and her breaths suddenly became shallow and fast.

He teased her sex, determined that nothing interfere with her enjoyment of their first time together. When her hips began to seek his touch more and more, he gently eased the tip of one finger into her, stretching her gently.

She gave a little hiss of surprise and turned her face against is shoulder.

But then her fingers grazed the head of his cock.

Luc uttered an oath and thrust toward her hand.

Inquisitive eyes met his and soft hands teased his length.

Luc sat up quickly, ripped off his coat, waistcoat and cravat, and pulled his shirt over his head. Yvette's eyes when he turned around had grown impossibly wide and her mouth formed a perfect "o" as her eyes took in his naked torso. There were more shocks to come for his shy lover, and it would not be easy for her in the beginning, he was sure. But he was a patient man. He'd make this good for her.

He lay down over her again and brushed her hair back from her face. "Is this all right, chérie?"

She nodded quickly and placed her hands on his chest. He suffered through a prolonged exploration before she smiled shyly and looped her arms about his shoulders. "Yes, Luc."

He moved between her legs, and his cock brushed her inner thigh.

Yvette lightly shoved him away again, her gaze darting to look between them at his arousal.

Luc held himself rigid, sure he was about to be sent away at any moment. He couldn't help how much she excited him.

But then a timid touch glanced across his length.

He gasped and clenched his fists.

"Did I hurt you?"

"Never, Mademoiselle Valiant." He pressed his lips to her ear. "Tease me again, chérie."

Her hand suddenly grasped his cock, awkward and unsure, but so unbelievably exciting to him. "You can touch me anywhere and any way you choose, and I'd never complain it wasn't enough."

Her touch on him became more confident and the torture was exquisite.

When her grip slipped away, he lowered his hips and slid against her body until he butted the head of his cock against the junction of the thighs. Yvette's arms encircled his shoulders tightly now, her fingers sliding into his hair. He was certain she was almost ready for him.

But just to be sure, he put his hand between her legs, toying with her clitoris expertly until her body was straining up for more than just his fingers. He dipped the tip of his finger into her depths a little.

Yvette gasped, a high and panicked sound.

He stilled, kissed her brow and slid back onto his knees, away from her. He had rushed her. "I'm sorry," he whispered.

She looked up at him, her hair in disarray, her chest heaving. "For what?"

"I can't help myself when I want you so badly."

She nodded. "I am too inexperienced for you."

"No, never. You're perfect just as you are. It's me that's the problem. I don't know how to do this any slower."

She suddenly laughed. "Sir, if you went any slower seducing me, we will be found out by your grandmother."

He nodded. "Can you forgive me if I hurt you?"

"Can you forgive me for being constantly surprised by everything you do?"

Luc nodded quickly and lay down over her again. "I just want you."

Yvette cupped his cheek. "This is all so different for me," she whispered. "You overwhelm me." She kissed him. "But I don't want you to stop now."

He nodded. "There are more shocks to come."

"I know. I've always known. I just thought

I'd not feel the same way as everyone else must."
She sighed. "Talk to me again."

"Cherie, amour. I feel so much for you my
heart might burst in happiness."

Yvette smiled and drew him back to her for a
deeper kiss. This time when his cock nudged at
her sex, she wrapped both her legs about his hips
and held tight to him as he slid home.

Her nails dug into his skin as she muffled a
hiss of pain. Luc quickly touched her clitoris,
giving it all his attention as he held still.

But Yvette was warm and tight and damp
with arousal now, and as she began to soften, he
couldn't help but start to move, too.

She caught his head between her hands,
staring into his eyes, and she smiled as they
moved together at last.

Luc watched her for signs of discomfort, but
she was with him, enjoying their loving the way
he'd hoped she could. He cocooned her in his
arms as they made love, never wanting the moment to end.

But it wasn't too long before Yvette's fingers
were digging into his skin as she gasped and
tightened on the cusp of her first release. Luc
watched her come, feeling awed and proud that
she'd chosen him to be her first and likely only
lover. He followed soon after, pulling her close as
his seed filled her with all his dreams, too.

Chapter Eleven

Yvette hummed a little tune and then blushed, while again attempting to hide her happiness. She was ruined after all. Thoroughly and completely by a terrible scoundrel named Luc Ayles.

But she couldn't be happier. Making love to Luc had been a wonderful experience. All that remained was for him to propose today and for them to marry. She was sure he had honorable intentions. He loved her, and she loved him, too.

Nothing could ever come between them now.

She couldn't wait to tell the world that Luc was hers, and she, his.

Yvette called for a maid to dress her, remembering last night's furtive dash back upstairs to her bedchamber, with Luc following not far behind fondly.

He'd not joined her in her bedchamber after they'd made love but had promised he'd be waiting for her the moment she showed her face outside her door today.

She wore her favorite gown and her best smile, then swept out to meet him…only to find an empty hall waiting and no Luc.

Disappointed not to see him, she went to the doorway of his room, wondering if he was still abed, but found it empty as well. He must have already risen and gone on with his day without her because she was later rising than she normally would be.

She moved to the head of the stairs and looked down, hoping to see him there below. For the first time since coming here, she did not feel dizziness when she leaned over the railing listening for his voice.

A door crashed shut somewhere below.

She shivered at the sound, but it wasn't from the cold. There was tension in the air that she'd never felt before. Worried that all was not well, she hurried down, glancing left and right as she reached the bottom of the stairs.

But those rooms were empty, too.

Troubled by that, and by not finding Luc waiting for her as he'd promised, she turned for the morning room where she ought to find Grand-mère at this hour.

Grand-mère was speaking French to someone inside.

Uncertain whether to interrupt, she waited outside, discreetly eavesdropping on the conversation to find out who was in there.

A lady was offered cream for her tea and another slice of bread and butter.

"Thank you," the answer came in easily understood English. "I'm weak with hunger today."

Yvette recognized that voice, and she pushed open the door to find her best friend sitting down with Luc's grandmother. "Charlotte?" she cried. "What are you doing here?"

"Saving you from a scoundrel's wrath, I believe," Charlotte said as she burst to her feet and hurried to embrace her. "Your brother is fit to be tied, I must warn you."

Yvette drew back from her friend's embrace. "Why would *you* leave the party, and with him?"

"Necessity. You cannot imagine the fuss your brother was about to raise over your disappearance. He threatened to geld poor Luc," she whispered. "I tried to tell him Luc would never have taken you against your will."

"Charlotte, I left of my own accord, because I was fed up with my brother's poor chaperonage."

"And my cousin left soon after you did. He left a note behind to say you were heading home to Bath, though. We would have found out it was a ruse sooner, had your brother asked more questions along the way."

Yvette winced. "My driver took a wrong turn. Luc wasn't following me, but he found me. Rescued me."

Charlotte grinned and looked around. "I knew you'd never come to a scoundrel's estate willingly, but he was sure he'd find you here."

Yvette frowned at her friend. "Is your mother here, too?"

"No," Charlotte said without meeting her eye. "I did what you did. I left her behind."

"Charlotte, what were you thinking to travel so far with my brother without a chaperone! Don't you know he's a scoundrel, too?"

"Well, I never asked for his company. He presumed to appropriate my carriage since you'd taken his. I merely didn't let him leave me behind."

The doors burst open, and Luc appeared, followed by a scowling Rhys. "I never thought you'd sink as low as this, to steal her away and send me on a wild goose chase, too," her brother was saying.

"There's a good explanation. Just let me fetch your sister from her bedchamber and—"

Rhys grabbed him. "You'll stay away from my sister from now on, you scoundrel."

That wasn't agreeable to Yvette anymore. She rushed forward to intervene. "Brother, if you'll let me explain."

"You stay out of this," he ordered, trying to grab Luc again.

She placed herself between her brother and Luc. "Stop this."

"I found her carriage stuck in a drift of snow," Luc argued around her. "I brought Yvette here to warm her up."

Rhys balled his hands into fists.

"Not a good choice of words, cousin," Charlotte warned as she threw herself at Rhys to drive him back. "Have you forgotten you are in the presence of ladies," she hissed. "You are making a spectacle of yourself."

Grand-mère sat by the fire, her eyes alight with excitement. "Do carry on shouting."

"As you can see," Luc began. "My grand-mother has been present to chaperone your sister the whole time. But do we need to talk in private Valiant?" Luc asked.

Rhys flexed his arms. "Indeed, we will. Outside."

Yvette didn't like the sound of that, but Luc immediately agreed, and the pair disappeared into the bright white garden.

She walked to the door, uncertain if she should follow Rhys in case he meant to harm her scoundrel.

Charlotte pressed her face to the glass, avidly watching the men argue outside.

"At least you know now that your brother does care, chérie," Grand-mère said with a laugh. "Such high spirits for so early on Christmas Day bode well for a good year to come."

"Oh!" she gasped. Looking at the old lady in dismay. In the excitement of her change of heart toward Luc, she had forgotten all about this being Christmas Day. And if Rhys could travel upon the roads, she feared she was about to be made to leave with him. "I don't want to leave with my brother," she attempted to say in French.

The old lady threw up your hands. "Oh, your accent is atrocious."

"I've had little reason to use the language before," she whispered, deciding to stick to English for now. "You're not angry with me for keeping it a secret that I sometimes understood you and Luc?"

"Did I not say you were a clever young woman?" The old woman shook her head. "Luc needs that, you know. He'd never be satisfied with a woman who couldn't keep him on his toes."

"I don't know about that."

"With a little practice, your French will improve, and you'll have nothing to be embarrassed about when you're introduced to the family as Luc's wife," she promised.

The last bit was said in French but Yvette understood her perfectly. "I hope so," she whispered, blushing under Charlotte's delighted stare. "But Luc has not yet asked me to marry him."

"He will," Charlotte promised, her smile wide.

"You knew all along he meant to marry me?" she accused.

"I suspected he preferred you, but I never dared hope you might return his feelings," Charlotte promised.

"Come sit with me, Yvette, and you too,

Charlotte," the old lady demanded. "No, sit over there, child, so when the men return, they must sit between the two women they love best."

Yvette blushed. "I could hardly believe he even liked me after how terribly I treated him."

"It did him good, not to have you fall swooning at his feet," Charlotte confided. "Affection comes all too easily to certain men."

"Make no mistake, my grandson is a scoundrel, chérie," Grand-mère warned.

Yvette smiled. "I know."

Madame Bisset shrugged one elegant shoulder. "I married a terrible scoundrel. Luc's grandfather was the most wicked of men. I enjoyed a very satisfying marriage bed." Her old eyes twinkled with pride. "I'm sure you will, too."

Yvette's cheeks heated as she remembered her night with Luc. He'd seemed satisfied by her first foray into wickedness with him. Of course, when they married, it would not be so wicked anymore.

The old woman caught her attention. "Now, I fear your brother is determined to separate you from my grandson. What lengths will you go to stop that from happening?"

"If he disapproves of the match…" She bit her lip briefly. Leaving Luc, her scoundrel, was the last thing she ever wanted to do now. "But I must do something."

"Then do it quickly, child, for they are already returning, and my grandson's shoulders are slumped in defeat."

Yvette gulped. There *were* ways to force a marriage. A stolen kiss being the least scandalous she could think of at that moment.

She hurried to meet her brother and Luc at the door. "Well?"

"All in good order. Provided the weather holds, we'll be on our way inside an hour," Rhys promised.

Madame Bisset called Rhys over to join her.

As soon as he was gone, Yvette looked up into Luc's sad face. "I'm falling."

Luc immediately gripped both her arms. "Let's get you seated."

"No. I'm not falling in that way." Her knees trembled. "It's the other way."

"The other way," he repeated…and then a slow smile crossed his face. "I apologize for not being able to remain outside your room this morning. Your brother arrived just as it sounded like you were stirring"

"I'm sorry, too," she whispered in French. "I had expected there was something you would have said to me before my brother arrived."

His eyes widened for a moment and then he laughed. "Always a surprise. It's one of the things I love about you. And yes, I did have a particularly important question to ask of you today."

"Mr. Ayles, you are too kind." She smiled up at him and fluttered her lashes. "How might I encourage you to ask it in front of my brother, so he won't take me home today?"

"Consider me encouraged and willing to fulfill your heart's every desire, chérie." He caught hold of her hand and then sank to one knee. "My dearest Yvette, my love, my everything. From the moment I first saw you twirl, I have been constantly challenged to be a better man to win your approval and trust. I should continue to strive for your respect and love for the rest of my life. Could I persuade you to do me the honor of becoming my wife?"

"My dear scoundrel. I would be honored to accept." She glanced toward the others, but her brother's back was turned. He'd seen and heard nothing of Luc's sweet proposal. So, she bent down and stole a kiss from Luc's eager lips.

Luc rose and drew Yvette into his arms. "I've waited so long for you. I burst to tell you of my feelings."

She beamed at him. "Well, I'm listening."

He took up her hands, raising them to his lips as he held her gaze. "Please believe that I love you and only you."

She touched his face and nearly cried. "I love you, too."

Luc caught her about the waist and twirled her round and round. She shrieked and held fast to Luc, but she was safe in her scoundrel's arms.

Rhys was suddenly by their side, dragging Yvette away from Luc. "What the hell is this?"

Luc only smiled. "I have permission."

Yvette scowled at her brother for his ill-timed interruption and rushed back to Luc's arms. "Rhys, this is not the moment to finally become a *good* chaperone. Mr. Ayles has just asked me to marry him, which I happily accepted, I might add," she confessed. "It's not my fault you weren't paying attention. So, go do what you usually do. Go flirt with Charlotte."

"Now that was rude," Rhys complained. He looked between them. "Are you sure about this, sister? There's no changing your mind."

"Rhys, I wouldn't dream of it," Yvette whispered. "I love him."

He gaped. "Well, why didn't you say that in the first place?"

"You never gave me a chance!"

Rhys thought about that a moment and then he grinned. "Excellent observation and all too true, I fear. It's not every day my sister is happy to have a scoundrel pursue her."

"Reformed scoundrel." Luc shrugged. "Forgive me, old friend, but I have important business to finish discussing with your sister. Do go away."

"As long as there's to be a wedding in the end, do carry on."

"And excellent idea, brother. Possibly the most sensible suggestion you've ever had." As Rhys preened at her praise, Yvette caught Luc's hand and waved her fingers at her future grand-mère and Charlotte before she pulled her future husband from the chamber to finish their discussion.

She took him to the drawing room where they'd made love the night before and shut the door on their family. She looked up expectantly at Luc's grinning face. "What happens now?"

He pulled her close. "If I leave for London tomorrow, I could return with a special license within a week to ten days."

She shook her head. "And risk having you come across some other damsel in distress, caught in a storm in need of rescue? Oh no. We'll return to London together, with Rhys to give me away and Charlotte as my bridesmaid. We'll be married there before my brother loses interest in my welfare entirely. I'm sure Grand-mère will understand the urgency I feel."

Luc laughed. "Practical and expedient. I've always liked the way you think," Luc murmured, glancing at the ceiling. "Now what is left to be decided?"

A smile burst from her as she looked up, too. Mistletoe had been amply added to the chandelier above them, and every high surface in the room. Luc must have arranged it after she'd left him last night. "Let mistletoe be your guide, my darling scoundrel."

He nodded. "You know there are distinct advantages to marrying a scoundrel."

"Such as?"

"I know exactly the kind of kiss you need right now." And then he proved he was a man of his word, giving her a sweet little kiss, and then another, and then a dozen more wicked ones indeed.

Epilogue

Two weeks later

Luc removed his spectacles and glanced across the carriage at his outwardly prim wife. They'd made good time from London, where they'd married by special license, and were unfortunately still hours away from returning to his estate, and his no doubt impatient grandmother. They'd promised to marry immediately and then spend the remainder of the winter holiday with Grand-mère celebrating in the country.

"Are you warm enough, chérie?" he asked.

"Almost."

Almost was not good enough for his wife. He put his book aside and lifted a corner of his thick blanket. "There's room for you here beside me."

"There's room for two on this side, as well, sir." She peered behind them. "Do you think Charlotte's warm enough back there with just her maid and my brother?"

Luc grinned. "Well, if she's not, she's no one to blame but herself."

"She didn't want to come between newlyweds. I hope my brother is behaving himself, too."

Luc smiled. "My cousin and your scoundrel of a brother are made for each other. Just you wait and see if I'm not proven right in the end," he urged.

"I hope you're right. I wouldn't want her to be unhappy."

"No fears for your brother, then?"

"My brother deserves every inconvenience that comes his way, and that includes a wife."

Luc laughed and moved across to her side of the carriage, tossing his blanket over both of them for additional warmth. He put his arm about Yvette's shoulders and drew her close against his side. "Better?"

She snuggled against his side. "I thought you'd never get here."

"I heard somewhere that a gentlemen should never impose on a proper lady in carriages."

"I'm not just any lady, sir, I'm your wife now," she warned.

"And a lovely one you are, too," he promised, then exaggerated a leer at her breasts. "So very delectable under there."

"Scoundrel," Yvette complained, but then laughed, cuddling up to him. "I don't remember it being this cold last time we traveled this way."

They had just passed the spot where they'd lost her brother's carriage, which meant home was still some way to go. "The first time you passed this way, you were angry with your brother and then at me, no doubt, for rescuing you from freezing to death."

"You were the last man I wanted to be my hero then. What an idiot I was!"

He kissed her brow. "My timing was perfect. I hate to think what might have happened had you gone on to Middleton's estate for help instead of choosing mine."

"I would have missed my chance to know there was more to you than a skirt-chasing libertine," she whispered.

"A man must seek affection where he finds it. If you'd refused to see my good side, I don't know where I'd have turned for comfort," he teased.

Her elbow jabbed hard into his ribs. "Only here."

"You're the owner of my heart now, true enough," he whispered. "But give me the kisses I need to be complete, ma petite. It's been so very long since our last. I'm desperate for you."

After a moment's consideration, Yvette wriggled around on the bench to face him, knees drawn up beneath her skirts. "Flattery like that will get you far in life."

"Further than kisses?" he asked hopefully.

"Perhaps."

In many respects, Yvette had not changed. She was shy of displaying her affections still. But in the carriage with the curtains drawn, perhaps she could be convinced that amorous activities with a husband were not so very scandalous. She could always say no, and he'd abide by her decision.

He bent his head to her ear to whisper, "Last night when we were in bed together, and you on top, I had the most delightful view of your pretty breasts and an urge to—"

She swiftly put her fingers over his lips. But not before he saw her eyes dilate with need. Yvette had enjoyed riding him in their bed. She'd tossed her head back as she'd climaxed and left him to find his own release when he could. She'd been magnificent in her passion, as he'd told her so many times on their journey today.

Luc was still a scoundrel to the bone, but the only woman he ever wanted to seduce now was the one who'd given her heart, soul and reputation into his care for safekeeping.

Yvette suddenly sighed a happy little sigh and whispered into his ear in French. *"Unbutton your trousers, scoundrel, and seduce me again!"*

More Regency Romance...

DISTINGUISHED ROGUES SERIES

Chills
Broken
Charity
An Accidental Affair

Keepsake
An Improper Proposal
Reason to Wed
The Trouble with Love
Married by Moonlight

Lord of Sin
The Duke's Heart
Romancing the Earl
One Enchanted Christmas

Desire by Design
His Perfect Bride
Pleasures of the Night
Silver Bells
Seduced in Secret

WILD RANDALLS SERIES

Engaging the Enemy
Forsaking the Prize
Guarding the Spoils
Hunting the Hero

*

SAINTS AND SINNERS SERIES

The Duke and I
A Gentleman's Vow
An Earl of Her Own
The Lady Tamed

*

REBEL HEARTS SERIES

The Wedding Affair
An Affair of Honor
The Christmas Affair
An Affair so Right

*

MISS MAYHEM SERIES

Miss Watson's First Scandal
Miss George's Second Chance
Miss Radley's Third Dare
Miss Merton's Last Hope

About Heather Boyd

USA Today Bestselling Author Heather Boyd believes every character she creates deserves their own happily-ever-after—no matter how much trouble she puts them through. With that goal in mind, she writes steamy romances that skirt the boundaries of propriety to keep readers enthralled until the wee hours of the morning.

Heather has published over 50 regency romance novels and shorter works full of daring seductions and distinguished rogues. She lives north of Sydney, Australia, with her trio of rogues and pair of four-legged overlords.

You can find details of her work at
www.Heather-Boyd.com